The Freak Within

By Millicent Courtney-Ware

D1528734

Ivy Pyramid Publishing

Ivy Pyramid Publishing
P.O. Box 11524
Fort Worth, Texas 76110
www.ivypyramid.com

ISBN: 0-9764634-0-7

Library of Congress Control Number: 2005900664

Credits:
Cover Conceptual Sketch Artist: Patricia Cass

Cover Design & Logo: Kaos Factor

Poetry, "These Past Six Months": Jason L. Ware

Printed in the United States

PROLOGUE

"Could you just come over for a little while? I know it's late; but, I need you..." whined Trey.

But, this whining and complaining has become all too familiar with the men in my life. I know you think that a girl should be such things as "grateful" and "appreciative" of all the attention. But, the truth of the matter is...it's boorish. So, refer to me as the "unchallenged one".

"Ari, I know that it's asking a lot, but, I would really like to see you tonight. I will even pick you up something to eat. Don't make me beg."

"I'm sorry," I say, "I'm just too tired. Maybe I'll catch up to you on Thursday when work slows down, okay? I'll talk to you later."

The simple truth is this. I have a much better offer on the table than Trey's. I already have an offer for dinner and intimate possibilities with Hunter. I will let you know right now that Hunter is much more than FINE. He is intelligent, sexy and, most of all, MARRIED! Now...I am not the advocate for indulging in adulterous affairs, but if you're gonna go to hell, why not get your toes curled one last time! I'm just kidding. I don't want to go to hell, but DAMN...

Anyway, Trey's the type that always wants you to come over to his place; and, he is more than happy to pick up anything you might want to eat: from the dollar menu. That serves its purpose when I don't have a more tempting offer on the table. He's cool and the conversation is good; but, his bedside manner isn't worth me making a late night trip to the other side of town!

I want you to know that the list doesn't stop there. I also have a few other special guy friends that I kick it with off and on. Now, just before you go and make assumptions, I want to clear up a common misconception or two. First of all, just because a girl has a few guy associates on hand, at any given time, doesn't mean that you change her given name or her standing in the community (if you get my drift). Secondly, I have not always lived by this philosophy. I once lived by a moral code that was stronger than the constitution because it couldn't be amended. But, now I stand as a changed woman. One could even consider it to be a different identity or a split personality-forever shifted.

There are a lot of things that I want you to understand. And, there are a lot of things that I am steadily learning about myself. I have the support of my family (on occasion) and two of my best "girl" friends that I secretly refer to as the "Angels." Not in Charlie's way, but in a good angel/bad angel form. I will leave it up to you to determine which category each one falls into. But, for now, just know that my girls (Kia and Phyllis) are really good friends, overall. Well, that's enough information about me for now. I will get some rest and let you see what tomorrow has in store for me, God willing...

CHAPTER ONE: MAINE

"We will bring this meeting to a close, since the projected forecast for our second quarter shows promise. Are there any questions or concerns before we adjourn?" I asked.

"I have a question, but, it can wait until directly after the meeting."

This comment came directly from Trinica Hughes; the finest sistah this side of blue collar land! Her downfall is that she plays too many games; just as she was doing right now.

"If your question pertains to our current business, then its best to state it now for the benefit of everyone present."

I knew this was one of her attention-getting tactics. She just loves a crowd. You would almost think that they were chanting her name the way that woman can carry on sometimes.

"No, it isn't. As a matter of fact, I answered my own question, thank you Mr. Richards."

I continue, "Well then, this meeting is adjourned and I will email you all with the minutes and time of the next meeting. Good day to everyone."

I had endured a long and exhausting night before this meeting, agonizing over the details because I always want to have my game face on. In fact, everyday that I go to work at CellCast, Inc. is a day for war. I am always apprehensive about one thing or another; and especially since my boy Julius got fired three months ago for banging most of the women on the 2nd and 4th floors of our office complex. I like to call it sexual harassment at its finest. I tried to tell him that keeping that many women happy was going to do him in one way or another. But, ego is the only incentive that he needed not to heed my advice. So, now, I am a lone wolf amongst the corporate sharks. At least having my boy with me gave me someone to bounce ideas off of and to check my "ghetto meter" against. Both of us being from the dirty-dirty South, you have to check yourself on occasion. But, sometimes, try as I might, the real nigga in me slips out.

For example, Julius had met this girl at a club that we frequent down in Atlanta,Georgia called "Come". It's pretty hot; and to go along with its name, the people who frequent the place are all card-carrying members of the Sex Fanatics Hall of Fame. So, you can see the possible penchant for our visits. Anyway, Julius hooks up with this lovely, lovely, lovely tan sistah by the name of Twice.

Long story made short, Julius and Twice had sex that same night and the night after that. Well, as you can probably guess, Twice was sprung on my man Julius! Just to give you a visual, Julius is about 6'2, 200 lbs. of pure steel and has the complexion of midnight. Hell, he's almost pretty enough for me to consider! But, all jokes aside (and all masculinity in tact), we are both heavy hitters in the looks department. As things usually go, Julius became cool towards Twice; having already conquered that mountain. But, Twice wasn't having it. She found out where my boy worked and would just show up for fake lunch dates; trying to arbitrarily catch him in the office and anywhere else he may be likely to frequent.

Well, on this particular day, Julius and I were at our barbershop on Throne Street called "Kutz". We were relaxing and listening to the latest gossip while waiting our turns for an available chair when in walks a bag lady off the street; scratching at her crotch and cursing under her breath.

"I know you didn't think I was gonna give you head and you wasn't gonna pay for it!" As she looks right at my boy Julius licking her ashy lips.

Of course, I am thinking, *"What the hell?"* Julius usually has a better looking clientele than this!

"I'm sorry lady, you must be mistaken," Julius stated simply; although it was becoming obvious that he was losing his cool. "There is one thing that I don't have to do-get street head from a crack head!"

The bag lady, obviously irritated by his remarks, started to point her finger in Julius' face and shouted, "You rich mothafucka's make me sick, especially you Julius!"

Right about this time, I noticed that the slim (also manicured) finger that had been poised on Julius belonged to none other than Twice Hall!

"If you think that you're getting away with anything by brushing me off, you're not," she continues, "This isn't the last that you've seen of me!" Twice hustled her way back into the street where she had come from.

"She must've forgot that Halle Berry already took that role in Jungle Fever," I said to ease the tension. At this point, laughter broke throughout the shop.

Drew, one of the barbers in the shop, told Julius, "Man, I don't want the type of problems you got! We trying to make sure we can renew our lease," giving dap to Ray, our barber.

"That bitch is crazy! But, I understand that the possibility of not having this dick at your leisure can be devastating! But, I'm through with her ass.

Nobody tries to clown me like that on my territory. Broke Bitch!"

We all laughed and continued with our talk. I think every brotha knows what its like at one point or another to have female drama; even if it was drama that you brought upon yourself.

I can remember a time in my life that drama was more appealing to me than to have peace. With each new chase, my boys and I would celebrate crushing some young girl's hopes. But, as it stands right now, that portion of the game has gotten a little old to me. I'm not saying that I want to trade in my playa's card for a wagon full of kids. But, there are times when I feel like there is something more out there for me. I'm at the point where I don't know exactly where I'm going; but, I'm leaving where I've been.

Just the other day, I had lunch with one of my long time friends, Ari Clayton. Now, Ari is one of those sistahs that has a lot of positive things going on. I love looking into those beautiful brown eyes and listening to her talk about life in her upside down world. You would think that the girl was from Australia the way she refers to the adventures that take place in the land "down under"! She is beautiful, educated and extremely sassy. There is one catch to Ari-you simply can't catch her. Whatever speed you are traveling, Ari is the type of woman that lives life on the Audubon. We've been cool for years; even worked together, at times. But, for one reason or another, the timing is never right. I don't really sweat the details because I feel that eventually she will fall right in my line of fire. Then, I'm going to shoot her ass just to keep her down! But for now, I have other matters to address of a more pressing nature. I need to find a flight into Monterey by tomorrow. I have some unfinished business that I need to attend to...

No more delay...

CHAPTER TWO: PHYLLIS

"Oh Lord, please help me to keep my legs closed; just as I promised you. Right now, I am under pressure and I need you."
I prayed quietly in the bathroom as I prepared for another night out on the town. I'm not sure if the Lord still has my line open; since I received a shut-off notice in the form of Chlamydia from my last praying episode. I really don't try to get myself in these situations, it just seems to happen. Dr. Phil had coached me on the love that I missed from my daddy as a child. The psychologist even told me to explore my soul and I would be sure to find the source of my misdirection. Kia and Ari told me that I was just too damn easy.

"But, I really do have feelings for him," I cried after I was diagnosed with the silent killer. "I was careful at first, but, he must have caught me slipping somehow!"

"Phyllis, you need to take a hiatus from sex, not only to cleanse your body; but to rid yourself of all of the internal drama. You know that they say that every time that you sleep with a man that he leaves his essence inside of you, among other things." Kia chatted on and on in regards to her friends downfall.

"You act as though I am a streetwalker, Kia! Damn, lighten up! I seem to remember some of your drama from the not-so-distant past, as well."

I hate for someone to preach to me; especially when their bible was missing a few pages. I think that the issue lies not in my daddy's lack of affection or my sexual tendencies, but in the fact that I'm in love with the idea of intimacy. I want it...Have wanted it all of my life. What woman doesn't? But, I am criticized by my judge and jury for not being a sexual prude. That's why tonight is a celebration of me. I am celebrating the fact that I have had 30 days sex-free!

Tonight, my girls and I are going to paint the town and feel good about being women.

"Bzzzzzz...It's me, girl!"

I hit the release on my door and let Kia in. "Oh girl, you are going to break backs tonight in that dress!" I said.

"Thank you, Phyllis. I have been working out for 2 weeks to make sure that I could fit into it. I just pray that it captures all of my...assets." Kia stated as she twirled around sticking her butt out. "Plus, I'm not about to let ya'll show me up. I know both

11

of ya'll went out and shopped for your man-catcher outfits specifically for tonight," Kia claimed.

Just then, Ari buzzed to announce her arrival.

"Hey ladies," Ari sighed as she sauntered in the room wearing her man-slayer attire. "I think we are about to hurt 'em tonight! In fact, I think we look too good for Misha's. Tonight, we should try that trendy new club, instead. What's it called?"

"Come," I said, knowing this is just the devil toying with me by putting this place into the mix. I've heard that it is really classy; a lot of suited brothers with degrees and pedigree hanging out in there. Well, if you ladies are ready," I said, "Let's do it!"

We all filed out of the door and into my Grand Am. I wanted to get our minds right. So, for the ride to the club, I put Javier into the sound system and we all rode and chatted. But, as we were riding, I couldn't help but think about all of the drama that has surrounded me over the last year.

Sometimes, I feel as though my life is passing me by; while I'm cruising along on auto-pilot. There have been too many days/events/faces forgotten. *What am I really doing?* And, don't think that I have forgotten about my little diagnosis. That is just the latest in a string of dramatic activities for me.

I know that you are probably thinking that I am acting a little too cavalier over just receiving VD from some man-whore. However, I am tripping on the inside; I just can't let my girls know how much it has really gotten to me. Have you ever slept with someone just because your body told you that it would be a good thing to do? Well, I did just that when I got with Kirby Alexander.

I guess you can call me a sucker for a smooth talker. Because that's exactly what Kirby did well; among other things! I was just exiting stage left from another relationship when I met Kirby. At first, I could tell that his interest was piqued because he smiled a lot and had a lot of conversation for me. I met him at the bookstore where he worked part-time and found out that he was a musician with a very popular local band called The Haymakers. I can't lie and say that my first thought when he told me this little piece of information wasn't "starving artist". But, I quickly got over that when he came from behind the counter and bent over to pick something up off of the floor. Kirby had the type of ass that one would fiend over and is usually seen on the football field. He also had the legs to boot! So, I forgot all about his occupation and started making the moves necessary to land him with his seat in the upright position! I batted my eyes and laughed in all the right spots and slipped him my personal card; the one I use when I really want someone to be able to get in contact with me. He called me that night when he got off from work and we talked until the sun came up. So, you know he scored immediate points for showing a sense of urgency and for his ability to keep up in his verbal skills!

I learned that Kirby played the Sax-all of them; which meant that he was not only good with his hands, but his tongue action was on point, as well. So, he made plans for us to meet at his place the next night and we were to go to dinner from there. So, I went to Rainbow to get me an outfit with some stretch to it to show off my curves. I came home in enough time to shower and curl my hair and I was off and running on pure adrenaline. By the time I made it to Kirby's place, I was all wound up and looking for something to level me off. I guess that's a bad place to be when you are trying to get your life together. I made it to Kirby's house in about 20 minutes. When he opened the door, I started looking around for the angels because I knew that I had died and gone to heaven! He had on a nice fitted white t-shirt with a pair of matching linen pants. He smelled of Issye Miyake; which I happen to adore on a man.

"Hello Phyllis, you look stunning," he said and smiled invitingly.

I don't even think that I said anything to him because by the time that I brushed past him to get into the door something just sparked between us. The next thing that I knew, I was caught up in an embrace that made me lose all control! Kirby kissed me softly on my lips; taking his time to suck each one into his mouth. His grasp on me was firm, massaging away my longing to feel a man so close to me. Kirby let his hands slide up and down my back; then lowering them to my hips while he pulled me into him even closer.

"Wait," I found myself saying or at least I thought I had spoken aloud.

Apparently not, the next thing I know, Kirby sank to his knees; while still kneading my thigh and calf muscles and began to lick my "mystery" through my stockings. I didn't have on any panties and I was thankful for that! I have never felt anything that felt as good as a wet nylon massage over my clit! I was so wet! Kirby began making slurping noises like it was the best meal he had had all day.

"Phyllis, I want you to relax and let me take you wherever your mind wants to go tonight," Kirby whispered softly into my ear as he held both of my arms above my head and slipped my dress over my hands.

He then clasped his hands into mine and began to make me rub myself as he guided my hands over my hard nipples, down to my pelvic region and up my sides. Then, he released his hold on me and began to kiss me from behind, biting me slightly; just the way that I like. By now, I am flowing like a good jazz song. I can feel my wetness traveling down my inner thighs.

"Oh baby, I am loving this…take me as far as you can go," I said; and with that, Kirby scooped me into his arms and carried me to his bed.

As he climbed on top of me, he asked, "Have you ever seen ecstasy?"

Slightly confused, I looked at him with a puzzled expression on my face.

"Just close your eyes, I don't want you to miss a thing," and Kirby entered me with a steady forcefulness. I'm talking about the kind that makes you wish you were a cheerleader in high school just so you could open your legs that much wider to receive such a gift.

"UH…UH…hoh…," I heard myself breathe.

Kirby kept a steady pace as he fucked me slowly. As I kept my eyes closed, I actually saw things that I never had before. At that moment of recognition, I realized that my body was betraying my mind as I was telling it not to come…At least not right now. Kirby leaned over and sucked on each of my nipples alternately and I let go of my carnal ghost. As I came, I opened my eyes to meet his in his moment of truth.

"This is the best shit I've ever had!" he said with more than certainty registering across his face.

I felt his stomach tighten and his release. We laid there exchanging looks of satisfaction, lust and respect for one another's skill. I soon fell asleep; only to be awakened at 6am by his alarm clock.

Kirby lazily reached over and turned it off. "I'm sorry, he said, "I have an appointment this morning at 7:30am."

I took this as my cue to get into the shower and redress. I did that and he took his turn in the shower, respectively. I made a mental note that he was still as fine as he was the night before. We did very little talking; since he seemed preoccupied with his daily plans. We both finished getting ready and hugged and kissed goodbye; with him promising to call.

At last, I was left alone with nothing but my thoughts and the memories of the night before ringing in my head. I called my job to let them know that I would be in later this morning. So, I went home and prepared to begin the professional half of my day. Not giving much thought to the events of the previous night; except how good it was, until 2 days later when I started having serious stomach pains. They were in my lower abdomen and were pretty consistent; as well as my loss of appetite. I didn't think much about it except for the fact that I knew that I had just had my period a week before. So, I was expecting no types of pain in that region for at least another 3 weeks. This went on for another week and a half and then I decided to see my doctor and find out what was going on. Dr. Hinton dropped the bomb on me and my mind went racing back to the night with Kirby that I floated in the ocean of love without so much as a wet suit.

"Dirty bastard!" I thought as I envisioned cursing him out for the physical anguish he had caused me.

That's what I was discussing with Kia and Ari now. As they continue to do battle over my physical; as well as mental state of being, I have drifted to a time when you could fuck whomever, whenever and it was all good. I realize that I was too young to participate in it when it was all good; but, you can't hate a girl for dreaming.

"Phyllis, what are you going to do? You need to confront his low-down ass about this!" Kia shouted, disrupting my thoughts.

"I don't know. I'm not sure if he even knows that he has it. I hate to admit this; but, I'm not even sure if he gave it to me," I said.

I really cannot be certain. All that I know is that I have been inclined to have a little fun now and then. Knowing this, I had just had a little secret fun with

18

my ex-man Key, 3 weeks prior to this episode. Now, Key is a whole 'notha story.

You know some sex is just good to you because you have history behind it. I called Key up nearly a month ago just to see what he was doing. The short version of our story is this: Key was what I like to call a trisexual. He was whomever and whatever you needed for him to be. I know that you are thinking "trisexual", is that a real word? No, it isn't. But, it refers to anyone who will do try anything in the sex arena; even within the same sex. I can already see you raising your eyebrows like I am on some other level. But, believe me, Key was that good! I really didn't care about his "other" experiments in the bedroom. I'm getting wet just thinking about him. I better get to praying again...

CHAPTER THREE: KIA

"The drama in my household is endless. He has even stopped coming home on a regular basis. I'm ready to end it," my customer was saying.

But, I know that she is lying. Jackie has this fit at least once a month when she comes into the shop to tell me, and the rest of my patrons, about the no-good activities of her husband. The bad part about it is that one of my Wednesday clients has slept with him before! In fact, I think they still see one another on the cool. I have to remember not to let their appointments cross each other in the event either one of them needs to reschedule.

I am just glad that I don't have to deal with that type of drama at this point in my life. I wouldn't know what to do if I had to jump back into the rat race and compete with all of these other women for the few "good" men that are left! I think it is even scarier because I have learned about some of the pitfalls that I have managed to avoid through the lives of some of my friends; especially Phyllis. That girl has so many issues. I love her to death; but, she could stand to close her damn legs! Ari and I have tried giving her advice about her life and some of the unwise choices that she seems to continue to make; but, it hasn't done a bit of good. I would swear sometimes that her mother forgot to sit her down and have "the talk". Anyway, those are the breaks sometimes.

Today, I am booked solid with my appointments and I am pressed for time. While I am finishing Jackie's perm, I have Sandra and Juanita at the shampoo bowls. I could afford to have some additional help around here. But it is hard to find reliable help these days. The last girl that I hired was Melinda. Now, I was trying to be nice and help out the friend of a friend. I hired Melinda while she was still in Cosmetology school. I wanted her to simply handle all of my bookings, receptionist duties and shampoos and prep my customers to free up some of my time. Well, that was one of the biggest mistakes that I've made to date.

Melinda was more interested in acting like her name was on the door. She showed up late for work-Any time after I show up is considered to be late. Plus, she stayed on my business line talking to all of her friends. Running a social hour was not why I was paying her. Then, of all things, she had the nerve to get flirty a few times with Simeon; which I simply wasn't having! So, needless to say, Melinda no longer works at The Hair Refinery. That name sounds so classy, doesn't it? I love for my people to show class in all of their ventures; especially in business. I could have named the place "Three Snaps and a Circle Beauty Shop" but that isn't the type of image that I want to portray. Also, just so you know, I put it down up in here! Not to brag or anything, but, I won Innovative Stylist of the Year in 2000 and 2002, respectively. I should have won in 2001; but, trying to help someone else out, they ended up stealing some tips and working them to their own advantage. So, you know that won't happen again! I don't intend to give another woman the stick to beat me over the head with. They are going to have to come much harder than that to get to the kid!

As you can see, my shop is one of my biggest accomplishments. I have always been good at hooking up hair. So, I decided to spin it into a full-time business for myself. I have been in my own shop now for about 5 years and counting. I still need to get some other stylist, which I can work with, in here to help me out. The idea is to expand the shop into other areas. So, it won't matter what part of town you are in, you will still get served. I want to have a full service salon for my people. We deserve to get massages, manicures, pedicures, facials-You know stuff that most of us have never had the opportunity to experience. Well, enough about my lifelong dreams. In fact, Jackie is still going on and on about her low down husband and his latest adventures. She hasn't even realized that I'm not listening to her. Her stories are all the same anyway. She just changes the days of the week.

"Yeah girl, I feel you on that," I answer just to keep myself in the game. I have to make sure that I get everybody in and out of here in a timely manner because I have to make cupcakes for Casey's birthday party at school on tomorrow.

Casey Marie is her momma's other pride and joy. I never really thought about kids until I found out that I was pregnant. Simeon and I have been married for the last 6 years and Casey is 5; so, I will let you do the math on that one. I can tell you right now that Simeon DID NOT marry me because I was pregnant with her. However, I do feel that it did do something to solidify the deal.

Simeon and I dated for about a year and a half off and on, more on than off. He was really cool. I liked him from the moment that I met him. I just wasn't looking to get into a serious relationship until I was like 35. Don't ask. It was just a number that I had in my head for things to sort of start working themselves out and come full circle in my life.

I was doing an internship in a shop across town called Miracles. Simeon was a courier for a mall service on that side of town. So, I would get a chance to check him out often. He even delivered to Miracles; which had to be one of the higher points of his day. Whenever he came by the shop, which usually happened between 2-3:30pm each weekday, someone would have some little fly quip to float his way. There were no bones about it. The on-the-job workout that he was receiving was doing his body good. Simeon's body was and is like a chiseled piece of chocolate. He must've been part of the Malik Yoba-Bald Men Are Sexy Movement because he was working that angle as well.

I kept quiet for a while; just watching his moves and how he handled the constant harassment from some of the more desperate, horny clientele that we had in the shop. He always seemed to be flattered by all of the attention that he received. I also noticed that he had a quick wit about him, too. I laid in the cut and watched the drama play itself out over several weeks.

One of the regulars, Dru, was always talking about what she was going to do once she got her hands on him. Dru wasn't a bad looking girl; she just didn't have the sophistication to get the job done right. You know, everyone has that girlfriend or some broad that they know that always has her game face on; but, she is always showing her hand too soon in the card game. Dru was that type of sistah. I thought she was cool and all; but in competition, Dru couldn't pinch hit for the kid! I sat back and watched her make her shots; albeit, most of them were in the dark.

I remember one Friday afternoon; Simeon had come to make a drop and a pick-up at Miracles. Dru had finished getting her hair done and was lounging around shooting the breeze with myself and some of the other patrons and stylists in the shop. Simeon came in smiling and speaking to everyone.

"Hello Ladies, who wants to give me a signature over here?"

"I'll give you something you can put your name on for me," Dru spoke in what I perceived to be her sultry voice. "Whatever you are giving, you can certainly pass that my way!"

"Well, well...Is there anything that you won't turn down?" Simeon smiled and asked Dru.

"Well, I would be a fool to pass up on anything short of a good time now, wouldn't I?" Dru asked coyly.

By this time, their banter died down because Rose had come up front to sign for the packages and to take care of the remainder of her business. At that time, I walked by Simeon, Rose and Dru to get some more products from the front storage closet.

"Hello," Simeon spoke to me; looking after me as though he saw something that he wouldn't be able to let get away.

"How are you doing?" I asked, noticing the daggers that had started to form on the back of my smock from Dru. I didn't wait for an answer from him as I went to the closet and proceeded outside to my car to get my new Jaheim CD from the player. By the time I turned around to shut the car door, I nearly ran smack into Simeon; who was standing there with an expectant look on his face.

"Could you sign right here, please?" He asked as he handed me his clipboard with a piece of paper that had a space for a name and a phone number on it.

"I don't see any packages with my name on them. I can't claim something that I haven't received," I said boldly.
Since he started this game, I was going to show him how it is played.

"Do you have faith?" He asked. "Because there are times that you've got to believe in what you cannot see," and with that, he pushed the clipboard back to me.

I had to admit, he was pretty quick on his feet. So, with that, I gave him my number and sent him on his way. He got into his van and drove off into the sunset or afternoon heat, I should say. I smiled to myself and went back into the shop to finish working.

"My, my, Kia. What did Mr. Dark-N-Lovely have to say that was so entertaining?" Dru asked me as soon as I darkened the door to the shop.

"Good girls never tell," I said, dodging the questions and her assuming glance all at once.

Well, let's just say that the rest is history and I won the man and missed the bonus round. This is not to say that I haven't had my share of ups and downs in the last 6 years. Did I not mention that my husband was and still is extremely fine? Well, that by itself is enough to buy a woman a lifetime of problems. I try not to worry about it because I haven't had much cause for concern. I must say, I am no scab by a long run. On even a bad day, me and all of my girls can give any woman a run around the block and still come out looking like Queens. But still, any woman worth her salt has to stay on top of her game if she still intends to play; and lately, Simeon has been excessively moody; even for him. I'm not reading anything into it, but I can't afford not to look over all the details. Plus, we have had a lot of new tensions added to our lives with the new house and my new Jaguar. I just had to have it! So, I know he's working extra hard, as am I, to keep it all together. Not to mention, Casey's needs are increasing by the minute. I swear that girl goes through shoes and clothes like nobody's business! But, you know that just means that I have to step up my game to keep my baby looking her best. We can't have daddy's girls lacking in the fashion department, now, can we?

CHAPTER 4: ARI

Right now, I need to do two things. First, I need to get my head together so that I can complete this proposal. This proposal has been hanging over my head for the last 3 weeks and I have waited until the last minute to address it, as usual. I think sometimes I love to live under pressure. Secondly, I need a good masseuse. I haven't had a good rub down in ages! I prefer to have men perform these delicacies; but, it is so hard to find a man that is well versed in the art of professional massage therapy that doesn't try to talk you into taking part in his personal body wrap! You know that I am speaking from total experience, as only I can, on the matter.

Once, I picked up an ad outside of Kia's salon that advertised such services. I thumbed through it and came across a color photo of an extremely handsome guy by the name of Adonis. Adonis was offering a special on his services and offered everything from therapeutic deep tissue massage to thermal wraps. So, I couldn't pass on a brother with obvious skills and the willingness to bring his services to you. What more can a sistah ask for??

So, I called his messaging service and left my information so that I could get that much closer to easing the pressures of my day. I left my cell phone number and awaited his call. I continued to run my errands; and, about 2 hours into it, Adonis called me back. I will just let you know that he sounded so sexy over the phone! His voice was like melted chocolate being poured over my bare skin. It was delicious! So, I asked if he would be able to see me today. You know I am not trying to let my stress linger any longer than it has to.

"Well, let me check my calendar, hold on a moment," Adonis replied. "No, I'm sorry. This afternoon and this evening are all booked up. I can take you on Friday evening around 6:15pm; if that's alright with you?" He asked.

It wasn't alright with me; but, I didn't have much of a choice if I wanted to treat myself to the hands of a God for an evening.

"OK...My name is Ari Clayton and I can give you the directions to my home," I said.

Two evenings later, I found myself in my den on top of the massage table with Roy Hargrove playing in the background. I don't know if you've ever had the chance to experience it; but, a good massage will do wonders for your over all well-being. Not only will it remove toxins from your body (once you've had the appropriate amount of water), but it will make you forget all of those things that cause wrinkles, crow's feet and frown lines. I opted for the deep tissue treatment because I felt as though I needed the rough handling that only it could bring.

Adonis was great! He took his time and applied the right amount of pressure; and even told me to tell him when to give more or less. I love a man who's trainable! Anyway, he worked my body over and then some. I never knew that an hour and a half could seem so short. But, there are no complaints from me. At this point, I must shake my head at you because I know that you thought that I slept with him, didn't you? You ought to be ashamed of yourself! Believe it or not, even the freakiest of freaks exercise self-control and restraint at some point. I will let you know that I could've gotten him if I would've wanted to; but, I simply wanted the pleasure of a man's strong hands roaming over my body without sexual complications. But, I will not deny the massage awakening those special stirrings in my lower region. That's the only thing that I hate about the situation. It presented me with another situation! Once I get that feeling, I have to cater to it; or, it won't go away. I will think about sex until I can satisfy the urge. So now, I need to find someone who's willing to help me out. This isn't the challenge, really. Someone is ALWAYS willing. But, as promised, I must keep my game face on and get to that proposal that is due.

I need to come up with a plan that will provide additional funding to the spec arts division of an engineering firm. This is not exactly my idea of fun. But, I do like the alternatives that consulting has to offer. I can't conceive nor remember the days of the 9 to 5 grind. I have chosen to blot out that part of my memory because it was only 2 years ago that I was doing just that. I am thankful that I was able to spin a few years of education, working too many other countless jobs and some decent connections into something that I can do to make a decent living for myself. Now, don't go and get the wrong idea. I am not high-capping; but, I can afford not to sit in the nose bleed section; if you get what I'm saying. Anyway, I better get back to being brilliant for a few hours. There is a conference call of accountability that I have to be on tomorrow and I must have all of my ducks in a row or else they are going to pull the plug on my pond.

I received the phone call this morning from the agency.

"We appreciate your work on this project; but, the risk involved in the venture that you've outlined is far greater than we are able to take at this time," Tim Atkinson, Implementation Specialist for Gordon Enterprises, told me.

Actually this is code for "we have found one of the good 'ole boys or his sons to work for us". Even though I wasn't especially excited about the work itself, I was excited about the hefty check that this work would bring. Landing the larger accounts makes a difference between nickel and diming your way to the next big payoff; or, having the opportunity to chill for a second and catch your breath while you renew your creative juices. I must admit, I am more than a little disappointed in their lack of ability to recognize talent. But, I will never admit that to them. As far as they know, they are one on a long list of clientele that I do business with. Plus, I have a business luncheon with a potential client that is definitely promising.

I met him through Barb Castanova, a longtime friend and former co-worker of mine that has proven to be essentially valuable to me during the time that I've known her. Barb is about 47ish (she never tells her real age); and, she has a hand in the

Telecom industry that has afforded her the opportunity to make some nice investments and increase her portfolio.

Barb is the type of woman that you would assume was on the cheerleading squad in high school and the most popular sorority in college. We started out vying for the same consulting job, 2 years ago, when I was first starting out on my own in the industry.

Barb had prior experience and I was the new kid on the block. We were competitors, but, we also had competition from some of the other individuals that were out to make a name for themselves in the corporate consulting realm. One day, the firm had all of its potential consultants in for a breakfast meeting to discuss our proposals and to see which one of us they would rather do business with on a long term basis. I was a little intimidated by all of the obstacles that I was sure that I was up against; that is, until I saw some of the proposals that were being presented before mine. This boosted my confidence in a major way. So, when my turn came, I attacked my presentation like an opponent in a championship fight. I felt certain that I had knocked everyone out-the first time out the gate.

And along came Barb. She was polite and candid in her approach. When she finished, she left uncertainty as a roommate with my otherwise confident spirit. This woman had clearly done her homework and then some. At the end of the day, we ate dinner at a nearby restaurant and celebrated her victory and my lesson in humility. From that point forward, she took it upon herself to mentor me and help me to get my feet off the ground. The woman was so gracious that she let me act as a co-consultant on the very campaign that I had lost!

Professionally, Barb has been a true God-send. Thus, that leads to my lunch meeting with Thompson Sanders.

Thompson owns and operates a software engineering firm that is looking for some ways to creatively; yet cost-effectively, bolster their marketing segment. When Barb introduced Thompson to me at a local art gallery, I must admit, I got wet right on the spot! He had the most sensual way about him that any man I've known has ever possessed. You could tell that the man is well put together: nice car, tailored clothes, expensive (yet alluring) colognes, etc.

Now, I am not saying that Thompson is built Ford Tough or anything; I am just saying that you can tell that he and the finer things in life have been introduced on a first name basis and they kick it together on the weekends.

"I have a reservation for 2…the name is Clayton," I said as I reached the lobby entrance of the L'adelaide Mansion and Hotel. This is one of the most breathtaking spots for dining clients that we have in the city. I use it quite frequently; especially for my higher end clientele.

"Your party has arrived, Ms. Clayton. Let Janiere show you to your seat," the hostess said.

I was more than impressed. I was ten minutes early in anticipation of his arrival and he had managed to get one up on me in that category. I noticed that I was being led towards the private meeting room in the back; the one that overlooked the river.

"Ms. Clayton, it's nice to see you again. You look marvelous," Thompson said as he stood to acknowledge my presence.

I smiled and exchanged the same pleasantries with him. I noticed that he had taken the liberty of ordering some fresh fruit. Nice touch.

"Mr. Sanders, thank you for meeting with me today. I know that your itinerary is overflowing; so, I will be sure to make the most of the time that I have. I brought along a binder to briefly introduce the ideas that I have developed for your company," I said; pulling my material from my briefcase.

"That won't be necessary; I am in no hurry today. I would really like to enjoy the beautiful display that has been put before me...and the food too," Thompson said, smiling in a slightly flirtatious manner. "I mean, I like to get the chance to know the people that I'm going to be working with. I don't want to just rush right into the formalities; so please, relax and let's order our drinks."

At that, I did unwind a little bit and ordered a white wine. The fruit display at the table was almost too beautiful to eat...I did say almost. We ate and talked about some of the movies that were currently on the big screen. Before I knew it, an hour had gone by; with no talk of the intended proposal having taken place.

"Oh, we are certainly going to have to do this again Ari," Thompson stated simply. "I have enjoyed your company immensely. I find you to be a refreshing addition to my team."

I smiled quizzically and said, "I didn't realize that I had been given the job. You haven't even looked at my introductory offerings for your company."

"I have a feeling that there are more proposals on the table than the present. I like the way that you carry yourself and that is enough for me to know that I want you on the team. Call my office next week and we will work on some of the details," Thompson told me.

And with that, he stood and extended his hand to me, took the check to the wait station and left. Now, I don't know about you; but, I don't know exactly what I have just gotten myself into...But, I do know that it certainly more than makes up for my loss on Gordon Enterprises; with some to spare. Oh, Adonis??

CHAPTER 5: SIMEON

The past is a bitch that sneaks up on you in the middle of the night, clocks you in the head with a tire iron and leaves you for dead. I just don't understand it. We all have one; and, at some point, it is going to boot you square in the ass. I tried to tell my boy Trent that his game wasn't as tight as it needed to be; especially when dealing with a woman like Tamara.

Trent is a co-worker and good friend of mine. We've been friends since we met in high school. My wife hates his ass. Probably because she knows how trifling Trent can be at times. My boy has good intentions; but, somewhere between good intentions and the honorable thing, he gets off track.

The latest scenario all started when Trent started making deliveries to a new division in town called the Gates Inn. It is a suburb of the city and a lot of new homes are being developed in that part. Now, being in the delivery industry does have its advantages and disadvantages; depending on who's looking at it. It allows you the opportunity to get out and spread your wings. You're not confined to a desk job. But, the manual labor can wear on you;

especially on those days when you don't feel like dealing with it.

Well, Trent started delivering to the Gates Inn. Most of his packages were just standard deliveries; nothing major. This is until he began to make deliveries to Sonita Willis.

I knew from the moment that he told me about her that, one day, we would have to sit down and discuss his will. Sonita ran a lingerie shop from her home. Now isn't that just asking for trouble?

We all have had stories about the occasional inappropriately dressed female that answered her door with her assets on display or something along those lines. We have all had the invitation to come inside from the weather and have a cup of coffee or some other hot beverage. Don't think that all of these offers are as alluring as they sound because most of them aren't.

Trent happened upon one of the more appealing ones. Sonita is about 5'7, caramel skin and the type of body Victoria Secret's prays to have advertising their goods. I'm not going to lie. I would fuck Sonita. I would bend her over and show her all of the components of a special delivery! She's that type of woman. The kind that your wife should never know that you know someone like her; on even a friendly basis.

Well, back to Trent. One day, many months ago, he was making a delivery of several huge boxes to Sonita's home/business. Of course, he has to go in and help her set the boxes up; since she needed a pallet jack to complete the delivery of all of the crates. From what he told me, Sonita was wearing a sheer cream-colored lounging suit that left nothing to the imagination. He could see her hard nipples through the fabric. He could even see that she believed in manicuring the pussy.

After he gets all the boxes into the storage area in the back of the property, Sonita hands him a smaller box and said, "This is for you. I want you to think about my offer. It's inside. Open it later and let me know."

Trent was as happy as a boy scout at this time and he couldn't wait to run back to the dock at the end of the shift and tell me all about it.

"I got a gift from Gates Inn today. Want to see what it is?" He asked; knowing full well that I wanted to know.

So, once we finished unloading our trucks at the end of the day, we went over to his Suburban and cut on the A/C, some music and opened the box. Inside, there were a pair of silk hand ties, a pair of silk boxers and a note that read: "I would really like for you to model these for me…Call me to set up an appointment 777-9311."

"So man, what you gone do?" I asked, playing the devil's advocate.

"What would any playa in my position do? The woman is asking for something and we all know that I never like to leave a woman in need of anything," Trent responded.

"What about Tamara, man? You know she gone act a fool if she finds out that you have pulled some bullshit," I reminded him.

"Tamara doesn't need to know all of that. All she cares about is when I'm gone give her some more money and when am I gone give her the dick. I ain't married to her crazy ass no way! I'm gone see what Sonita is talking about. For all that we know she might want to put a brotha down on her team on a full time basis!"

That is what was known as the beginning of the end for my friend Trent. Sonita introduced my man to bondage and any other freaky shit she could think of. I knew that this was not going well when she started taking pictures and video footage of their activities. Now, I know that I don't know all the rules to the game; but, I do know that you do not let anyone take compromising footage of you. What was once considered fun now becomes evidence against your ass. So, in order to spare you the bulk of the details, I will give you the short version.

Tamara began to suspect that Trent was up to no good. Because you know that he was so knee deep in Sonita, that he wasn't being the most cautious person with his whereabouts; or, even bothering to come up with good explanations for his absences. So, Tamara began to start following my man to see where he was going on those occasions that he made up an excuse not to be with her.

Well, one night, Trent took Sonita to a place called "The Dungeon." This hideaway is known to be a place where people who are into sexual alternatives hang out, eat and whatever else they can come up with for the time that they are there. I don't know what happened while they were in there. But, according to Trent, they were all smiles when they left the place. That is, the kind of smiles that say "these two people are about to get buck-naked as soon as they get in a dark space" kind of smiles. Well, that is, until Tamara jumped out of the bushes near Trent's car and slammed a brick through the passenger side window of his Suburban!

"Bitch, I'm gonna kill you...You gone have to pay for that!" Trent yelled at her disgusted that she had damaged his new ride.

"I might pay for it, but you ain't gonna kick it with none of these hoes no more!" With that, she bent over and shanked Trent in the knee with a rusty 6 inch blade! Sonita screamed and tried to take off running; only to be kicked in her back by Tamara's boot.

"That'll teach you to fuck around with Tamara's shit! Both of you sorry motha fucka's can kiss my ass!" Tamara sneered and took off around the corner.

Trent called me from the emergency room to let me know what had happened once his injury had been packed and stitched. This little stunt cost him 3 weeks off; plus therapy. To top it all off, Sonita refused to speak to him since it all happened. He pressed assault charges against Tamara as soon as he got out of the hospital.

But, since he returned to work on light duty, he started to receive anonymous packages of underwear in the mail with the words "Nasty Ass" written across the butt. HA! HA! Go ahead and laugh, because I sure did. I tried to tell him that Tamara was going to do him in when she found him out. So, needless to say, my boy is back on the dating scene with a limp! He has even had to change his route since he started back driving. Too many memories of the Gates Inn to go back to the way things were.

But, you haven't heard the best part of the whole story. Since Tamara and Trent were living together before their split; guess who he's rooming with now? I'm sure it isn't hard to figure this one out. I did say that he was my boy and my co-worker. I hate to see another man fall victim to the game.

So, this is my way of supporting the cause; at least for a little while, or until Kia threatens to put us both out.

CHAPTER 6: MAINE

Stepping off that plane was like stepping into another world. The heat and humidity were lovers; and there was no such thing as breaking them up. I decided that I was going to ease into things once I got here and check out the scene. I know that I said that I was ready to get down to business; but, I lied. I need to get a couple of good drinks in me and unwind first before I allow my pressure to rise.

I caught a cab from the airport and went straight to the hotel. I needed to shower and relax a bit before I changed clothes to hit the town. I came in the room and put down my bags to survey the room. I love it when my accommodations are just the way that I like them; big, roomy and clean. I can't stand to pay good money and then be scared to sleep in the bed because of all of the possibilities of foreign objects hiding in the covers.

That happened to me a few times in New Orleans. I stayed at some place that was recommended by a friend and I will never do that again. I think it was supposed to be a bed and breakfast; without the breakfast. I paid $150 for the night and I was pissed off when the place smelled like mildew and I was too scared to sleep under the covers because I knew I wouldn't be alone. So, this is so much better!

The sun is out and the day is beautiful. I asked for a room with a view of the onsite waterfall and park. This place is almost as good as any resort. I have another business associate who partners with the guy that runs the property; so, that's how I have been able to luck upon a place as nice as this one. Of course, coming out here brings out the wild child in me. I often imagine living out here and having a house built where my back deck faces the water. I also imagined having my house surrounded by sand and having nightly beach parties for anyone who happened to be in the neighborhood.

However, I need to wake up from this little dream because there are some other things that come with it that I need not think about right now. So, I got into the shower, toweled off and lounged in front of the 47" screen TV and let my mind wonder. I know that the sleep angel will be here soon enough.

But, instead of the sleep angel that I was so anxiously awaiting, it was Miguel at my hotel door.

"What's up, dawg?" He asked as he began looking around my room for signs of life other than my own.

"How did you know which room I was in?" I asked, knowing the answer.

"You know that Carmelita can't keep a secret. You should never make a reservation through her and expect no one to know you're in town," Miguel answered. "Now, how about putting on some clothes so that we can go over to the Cantina and have a few drinks to get you off to a good start?"

Since I knew that there was no getting rid of Miguel, I did just that. I got dressed and we headed over to the Cantina. I have known Miguel for quite some time. He and I had a mutual business partner a few years back that introduced us to one another. I thought it would be good for me to always keep different contacts in various areas in the event that I needed to spread my worth and move into new territory.

Cellcast, Inc. was small time back then and looking for new opportunities was one of the things that I was paid well to do. Miguel worked for another independent provider and had mentioned branching off and becoming a possible competitor against his company because he was not only the brains of the operations; but, the brawn, too. Miguel was well connected to many people; and a bad word from him may mean a not-so-happily ever after for someone else-if you lived long enough to see it through. So, needless to say, I have always managed to stay on Miguel's good side. Now, don't get the wrong idea; I ain't scared of Miguel or nothing like that. It's just that a man must learn to pick his battles more carefully if he is to live to fight another day.

So, Miguel and I are at the Cantina; which is a local dive that serves good food, good drinks and has some of the best looking women that hang out, as well as work there. So, that was another reason that I didn't mind going. Why not start off my trip with a full stomach and good scenery to boot? I listened to Miguel give me an account of all of his dealings over the last couple of months; both business and otherwise. That Miguel was one wild boy! I knew that he had one major downfall...women! I can tell how surprised you are at that revelation.

But, Miguel suffered his fate in the most miserable of ways. Miguel was married to Veronique. Veronique was the type of woman that made a man want to do the right thing. I mean, not that a man can't make that decision on his own; but, Veronique made you not have to go to your mental reserve to convince you that staying with her was the right thing to do.

Miguel and Veronique were married for about nine years and had a happy life together when it happened. Miguel messed up one night and slept with a girl that had been hounding him for years. Her name was Malisa Dominguez.

Malisa was fine, don't get me wrong; but, she had nothing on Veronique. I think Malisa's jealousy over someone else having it so well is what led her to pursue Miguel so tough. I have to give it to him- Miguel fought the good fight; but, he ultimately lost the battle.

One night, Malisa caught him slipping when she heard that Veronique was going to be out of town for a few weeks with a modeling gig. The way that I heard the story is that one night during Veronique's absence, Malisa showed up at Miguel's office and told him some story about someone stalking her; and how he was the only one that she knew that she could turn to for help. Supposedly, her stalker had threatened to come by her house and break in on her; so, she was too scared to stay there and needed the protection of Miguel. Miguel, being the gentleman that he is, stowed away some of his weapons and headed to Malisa's to put in work. Well, when he got there, she put on this act about not being able to sleep through the night knowing that "he" could come at any time. So, Malisa asked Miguel if he would stay over, on the couch, and be her lookout for the night.

Well, Miguel agreed and he stayed the night. Somewhere between the hot toddies that Malisa was making to keep him up and him falling asleep on the couch, Miguel awoke to find Malisa stroking his manhood and licking on his neck. Let's just say from there that Malisa worked her magic on Miguel; a magic that somehow ended up on tape (complete with audio) and that tape ended up in Veronique's possession! But, the story doesn't stop there. Of course, Veronique is furious, puts Miguel out and breaks off the relationship. I've been saving the best part of this story for last...Are you ready? Malisa is Veronique's sister!! Well, so much for a family reunion!

So, the short of their story is that after the divorce, Miguel has had a penchant for sharing the bed of relatives. Sick, ain't it? But, I think we all have our issues. The world would be a boring and mundane place if we didn't, now wouldn't it? So, at the least, I am going to begin my good time here with Miguel; and hopefully, try to keep him from doing something that will land us all in a lot of trouble.

While hanging out with Miguel at the Cantina, I ran into another acquaintance of mine by the name of Jeren Stokes. Jeren has been living down in Monterey ever since he still had dreams of playing pro football back in the day. Jeren moved to Monterey to be closer to his Arena team as he awaited the call of the pro scouts that never came. Jeren has done alright for himself, though. I was never one to get caught up in dreams, myself. I am a man who prefers my reality. Don't get me wrong, dreams have their place. But, I don't like dealing with disappointment.

I have spent the better part of my life dodging that aspect. It started with not disappointing my mother when she wanted me to say cute things that she taught me in front of her friends. It grew to not disappointing my dad and going to a "good" school and graduating with a "good" job. So, I think I have the dodging thing down pat. Up until now. There comes a time in a man's life when he can't run anymore; and bobbing and weaving are moves best left to the boxing pros. I am running out of time on this one.

CHAPTER 7: PHYLLIS

"Phyllis…callback on line 7."

I was at work and trying to get into the groove when I heard my name on the intercom. Well, so much for easing into the day! But, I can't complain, these are the type of calls that I love to get because they mean mama can take the bonus money and get herself a new pair of shoes! My job isn't too difficult. It has its hectic moments. Sometimes, I come to work and don't really feel like talking to strangers. You know? Do you ever have those days where holding cordial and friendly conversations is just too much? Sometimes, I just want the show to stop because my feet are too tired from tap dancing for the man 8 hours a day. Well, let me get this thing under way. It's time for me to earn my keep. I pressed the info button for line 7 so that I could begin my call.

"Hello Mr. Stratford; and thank you for returning my call. Which package would you be interested in today?" I asked the caller.

"I only called back to ask you how you got this number? This is a private access line," Mr. Stratford stated.

"Well sir, our database is taken from an undisclosed source..." I began to give off my scripted speech as the line went dead. Little does Mr. Stratford know that he will be called again by one of my associates since he didn't request to be removed from our call list.

Now, I know that such things as hang-ups and being cursed out are a part of a telemarketer's diet; but, I cannot say that my little chat with Mr. Stratford didn't change my mood somewhat. I like to feel as though the power to persuade is one that I am most expert in; plus, I had already planned to spend his money at the Shoe Warehouse on my lunch break. So, I guess its back to square one; or should I say the next call.

I dialed into the system and began to take incoming calls. I was prepared for the day because I had done my vocal cord exercises on the way in; and I was armed with my hot herbal tea. This job can be really hard on your voice if you're not careful. One of my co-workers named Celia always helped me out with tips on how to stay on top of my game on the j-o-b. Celia actually sits directly across from me; so, that leaves a lot of time for us to communicate throughout the day.

The new training class was just released onto the floor for training and Celia is one of the floor trainers on our team. I must say that sometimes the open office concept can be quite challenging. This is because of the fact that it lacks privacy.

One of the unique features of our cubed environment is that our cubes are made of clear Plexiglas; so, even though we are separated, we can still see one another. Now, where is the blessing in that? Well, usually it can be annoying; but today, I can definitely see the benefit-literally.

Celia is training a Hershey-colored brotha with the clearest brown eyes. He has a nice set of teeth and a full set of saxophone lips. I felt the heat rising just looking at him! My day was starting to look promising again. Now, I know that you are probably saying to yourself that he is sitting with Celia, right? Well, let's just say that I don't fear any competition from Celia. Don't get me wrong, she is a very attractive and well-bred sistah; not to mention, highly fashion savvy. But, Celia has been known to be a cat lover; if you get my drift. So, I put my phone on work mode, grabbed some papers and made my way over to Celia's cubicle. I could see that she was explaining some of the phone functions as I sauntered up; so, I figured it would be a good time to divert the student's attention.

"Hello Celia. I don't mean to interrupt; I just wanted to welcome our new team member. Hello, my name is Phyllis Deloy," I said sweetly.

"It's nice to meet you, Phyllis. My name is John. John Good bar," my new friend spoke.

I stood there stunned for a second. He didn't just say his last name was "Good bar", now did he? I had to commend myself for being able to spot a Hershey's product a mile away! But, I had to know the answer to my next question, also.

"You wouldn't happen to be related to Solomon Good bar, would you?" I questioned.

Hershey piped up. "Yeah, I am! How do you know Solomon?"

Now is the time for me to black out. This is more than awkward. *Can they still see me? Okay...yes, they can.* Alright, let me pull myself together and work this one out.

"Yeah...Solomon and I used to work together a while ago," I stammered.

"What's your name again? Phyllis, right? I'll tell him that I saw you today when I get home," John said.

He'll tell him about me when he gets home-Oh shit! That means they must be related!

"Okay, just tell him that I said hello," I said as I hurried off to the bathroom to get myself together.

I have to say that I am more than a little embarrassed to say this. But, I am going to be even more embarrassed if John gets cozy with Celia or any of my other co-workers and tells them what I am about to tell you. It is true that Solomon and I used to work together. But, it's a little more complicated than that. Solomon was my pimp.

A few years ago, I fell on hard times and I needed to dig myself out of a pretty big financial hole. A girlfriend of mine introduced me to Solomon Good bar and it changed my life as I knew it. Solomon took me in, put a money bandage on my financial wounds and made me forget all about the life of hard knocks to which I had become accustomed. Solomon was one of the sexiest men I've ever come in contact with; and, I worshipped the ground that he walked on. Not only did he lace me with money; but, he saved me from a potentially life-threatening situation with another guy that I was seeing at the time.

After hanging with Solomon for a few months, I was willing to give myself to him completely. I felt that the least that I could do was to repay the man for all of the trouble he went through on my behalf. And, I didn't have any money of my own. So, I offered Solomon the sex.

Can you believe that he turned me down? Now, it could've had something to do with the fact that I hadn't turned 18 quite yet. But still, no man that I know of would've told me no; and that made Solomon extremely noble in my eyes. So, 10 months later as a present to me, Solomon and I made love for the very first time. Granted, I was no virgin at the time that this all went down. But, Solomon raised the bar for my search for the ultimate sexual experience. Solomon made me feel so good about myself. Always telling me how sexy I was. I changed everything about myself for this man. I changed the way that I dressed, my hairstyle; even my whole outlook on life. I was in love and nothing could be better than that! That is, until Solomon started looking out for Sonya.

Someone that Solomon knew told him that she needed his help; and she clung to him from that point forward. Solomon still took care of me; but, I began to notice that, little-by-little, Sonya was edging me out. Solomon always let it be known that his business was private and you only involved yourself in what he allowed you to take part in. So, I only involved myself in the parts of Solomon that he shared with me. Private parts. He knew that I would do anything for him because I owed so much to him for saving me. I guess that's why he didn't have any hesitation in helping out more females in distress. I guess that also made it easy to ask us to perform for him, all of us together, on a weekly basis. I learned how to do things that I want to forget. I guess that's why I love dick so much to this day. I started out diving for pearls on the regular.   I know that you are asking yourself, "Where does the pimping come in at?" Well, just as an f.y.i. to you, all hoes don't walk the streets. Plain and simple.   If a man is paying you and you find yourself doing things that can't be reported in the church announcements on Sunday; he has become your pimp.

I saved some of the money I had gotten from Solomon and enrolled myself in college.   I took on work study jobs and moved into the dorm.   The day that I told Solomon that I was leaving was one of the hardest days of my life.   At that point, he told me how much he loved me; and, that he would always be there for me.   That felt good; and hurt me at the same time.

Now, here I am face-to-face with a ghost from the past; or, one of his relatives, and I am at a crossroad. Even though I haven't thought about him in years, my heart has always been in search of Solomon.

CHAPTER 8: KIA

"Hey girl, are you at the shampoo bowl or at your station?" Phyllis asked me. I could tell by the way that she asked that she had something she wanted to talk to me about.

"I'm doing a perm, so you got a minute. What's up?" I asked, cutting to the chase.

Sometimes I have to remind my friends and family that I still run a business. Just because you work for yourself doesn't mean that you should lack good business etiquette.

"You can't guess who started working at the Resort-Solomon's brother, John!" Phyllis shouted into the receiver.

Now, that's a name that takes a sistah back in time! I remember Phyllis being wrapped around Solomon's dick like she was liquid latex. But, that has been at least 10 years ago.

"Girl, no! Did he recognize you?" I asked.

"No, unfortunately I was close to the man; but not close enough to get to know his family. I didn't even know that he had a brother," Phyllis said sadly. "I don't know. It was just a trip that I would meet him after all these years. I must say, he is equally; if not finer, than Solomon," Phyllis continued.

"I feel you. But, I'm on my way to the shampoo bowl. Let me call you a little later on," I said.

"C'mon Shay, let me wash you out," I told my customer as we made our shuffle back to the shampoo bowl. To tell the truth, I really wasn't in the conversating mood; which I know is hard to believe when you work in a gossip den.

I suppose my mind was a little preoccupied from the phone call that I got earlier this morning from my sister Medra. I'm concerned that my little sister will never grow up and take responsibility for her life. For instance, just this morning, she called me crying to ask me if I had $400. She told me that both her phone and her light bill had gotten severely behind; and, she needed the money to prevent both from being cut off. Now, just two weeks ago, she was in the shop buying a bootleg Louis Vitton bag for $170 cash; not to mention the fact that I had just put a new weave in her hair for the family discount of $90! I swear, that girl's priorities are all wrong. But, just like I told her, I can't afford to take care of her and my family too. Plus, she is too damn old for me to file on my taxes! I told her that I could give her $100; which I expected to be repaid. Take it or leave it. Don't get me wrong; there is no better feeling than to be able to help out your loved ones. But, the Lord helps those that help themselves; and some of these situations can be helped!

"The Hair Refinery, this is Kia," I answered the phone from the shampoo bowl.

"Hey baby, how's it going?" My husband quizzed.

I sighed and answered, "Same old soup, warmed over. How's it going with you?"

"Alright...alright. I just wanted to let you know that Trent and I are going to hang out over at Bruce's place tonight," Simeon said. "I just wanted to let you know so you wouldn't make any other plans when you got off work tonight."

"Okay, baby. That will be fine. Just be careful and remember, there is an open container law in affect," I told him.

Now, I have never been the type of woman to trip over my husband hanging out with the fellas. I actually encourage independent activities outside of the home. I think it keeps a marriage fresh when you can go and have different experiences, within reason of course, and come back to the home front. It helps to get rid of bad stress; and, your relationship flows so much more smoothly.

61

By the time I get in tonight, it will be time to put Casey to bed. Then, I can get a little piece and quiet. Plus, I will practically have the house to myself. I will be "Queen of the Remote" for a few hours. Oh the joy! While I catch up on some of my shows, I can pull out my foot bath and give myself a mini-pedicure. Nah!! That's too much work. I'll just shower, sit back and do nothing. It is so seldom that I get to do that anyway. But right now, I haven't even made it over the midday hump and my day has been more than full already! I have 3 more perms, 1 head full of weave, 1 shampoo and a wig to fashion before I can call it a day. I don't even think that I even look at a day in terms of hours anymore. The type of styles that I must do determine how long I will be working; and today is definitely going to be a long one!

As soon as I got home, Simeon and Trent nearly knocked me down trying to get out of the door for the evening; which kind of made me wonder what they were really up to this evening. Ever since Trent moved in with us a few weeks ago, he and Simeon have been acting like they are back in high school. Sometimes, I find it funny to see them revert back to the ways that my husband only recently gave up. Other times, it can definitely test my nerves.

For example, the other night, I overheard them in the den comparing how many girls they hit when

they were in college. They were breaking them down into demographic categories; with emphasis on the graphic. It was really coming from Trent's end. I like Trent as a person and all; but, I have always had a low opinion of him from a dating standpoint. He has never been settled since I've known him. You would think that his current living situation would be enough of a wake-up call for him to survey his life and realize that its time to grow up. It hasn't been all that bad with him living here, though. In fact, he is rarely here most of the time.

But anyway, I'm listening to Simeon give an account of some girl he used to do back in the day when the doorbell rang. "Damn," I thought. So much for me getting the low down on some of Simeon's old dirt. I sauntered into the hallway and opened the door. I remembered that Ari was supposed to come by and help me with some graphics for my new logo for the shop.

"Hey girl! I stopped by Braum's and got us a little something," Ari beamed. My girl always knows what to do. Not that either of us needed the ice cream. It is just the principle. Every girl needs to have moments like these.

"Hello Simeon. Hello Trent. What are you guys doing with yourselves?" Ari asked as she entered the living room.

"Apparently not doing enough of what you doing! Girl you are fine as a b-ii-i-t-c-h!" commented Trent. "You know Ari; I could end your search for someone to warm your bed at night. All you have to do is ask."

"Yeah Trent? You would end my search for a bed warmer and start my search for your health card! I ain't even trying to add that type of drama to the picture," Ari smiled as she verbally lashed out at Trent.

Simeon joined in, "Shoot, T. You need to quit messing with Ari anyway. You don't have enough words in your vocabulary to get with her!"

"Alright...alright..Enough of all the bullshit!" I said. I knew that continuing this conversation was just going to get Trent bragging about how good he is and all of the stuff that he could put on my girl.

"C'mon Ari, let's take this into the library so that we can get started," I said to get things going in the right direction.

"What was that?" Ari asked as she turned around to walk out of the room. There was a quarter laying on the floor right behind her.

"I just wanted to see if your ass was tight enough to make that money bounce!" Trent laughed obnoxiously. I swear he was a trip.

"Simeon, you better get your boy! It's a wonder he ever gets any with lines like that," Ari said. We're all friends, so she really isn't tripping over how stupid Trent is.

"Girl, we have other things to do besides help Trent get his rocks off. I have some ideas that I want to show you for the logo. Maybe you can tell me how to make these work," I coaxed Ari.

"I'll take a look at what you have," she said. "And, I will let you see some of the designs I came up with from your ideas. That way, you can look over everything and choose one; or, we can come up with a different concept if you say that you like more than one idea," Ari beamed expectantly.

She is an extremely talented artist. I'm just glad that we are friends because I know that her work does not come cheap. I couldn't afford to pay her "for real" fee. So, it is nice to have friends who are going places in the world that will take a sistah along for the ride.

"I'm going to go and put the ice cream in the deep freezer while you get your stuff out and get set up,"

I shouted to Ari as I headed towards the kitchen. Just then, the phone rang.

"Hello?" I said into the receiver. Sometimes, I get so tired of the phone ringing.

"Hey, what are you doing?" My sister Medra asked.

"Ari and I are about to do some work for the shop. Why? What's up?" I asked half expecting the answer to be followed by a plea for more money on her part.

"Nothing much. I was just calling to see if you still had that diamond earring and necklace set that you got from Friedman's last year. I wanted to know if I could borrow it to wear it to a fashion premier that Jordan is putting on to benefit the center on tomorrow night. I just know that it would set my dress off!" Medra exclaimed.

I sighed heavily for only the second time today. At least this is better than right out asking me for more of my money.

"I'll see about it. But you better not lose it. That set isn't insured yet and I am planning to use it next week for myself," I lied. I just needed her to know that there will be none of that keeping my shit and acting like I gave it to her when I ask for it back.

"OK…no problem. I'll call you tomorrow and check and see what time I can come and pick it up. I'll talk with you later."

With that, Medra hung up the phone. I put the ice cream into the deep freezer and headed back toward the library so Ari and I could get started. Just as I was walking past the guest bedroom door, Simeon reached out and grabbed me by my waist from behind; planting nice, warm kisses on my neck.

"Do you have a minute to show a brotha some love?" He whispered into my ear.

Before I could answer, he pulled me into the guest bedroom, reached under my dress and pulled my panties to the side; proceeding to massage my nakedness. Next thing I know, I am being pushed backwards onto the guest bed as Simeon thrusts into me hard and quick.

"Take this dick like a good little girl and tell daddy how much you like it," Simeon panted.

When I went to open my mouth, I swear I didn't make a sound; at least not one that would be recognizable. I leaned into his arms and bit him on the shoulder. When I did that, he pushed into me so deeply that I became one with his spirit. Then, I came so hard that I felt my spine snap.

"Simeon, I…" I started.

"Shhhhhhhhhh...you've got company. Show me how much you liked it later on tonight," Simeon replied.

In one motion, he zipped his pants up and headed out of the door. I was left with my dress around my waist and a rapid heartbeat between my legs. I went into the bathroom to take a hoe bath and get myself together. I don't know what came over him; but, I liked it! Things like that don't happen very often for us anymore with our daily routines kicking our butts and taking names. So, I made one last assessment of myself in the bathroom mirror and ventured back into the hallway to the library.

"Girl, what took you so long?" Ari asked as soon as I entered the room.

"Nothing really. I just had to get something in the other room," I said sheepishly.

Ari raised an eyebrow. "Yeah. Whatever you went to get must've been worth fighting for. Where is your left shoe?" Ari asked; as I looked down to confirm that it was missing.

Now, you know that must've been some really good shit!

CHAPTER 9: ARI

"You have 4 new messages. First new message...received today at 7:45am...Ari, it's Trey. I was wondering if you weren't busy tonight if we could hook up. Call me later. Message deleted...Second message...received today at 9:10am...Hey Ari, its Trey. Are you free for lunch? I know McDonald's is doing their Monopoly game promotion and I won a free sundae and thought of you. Holla back at me. Peace...Third new message received today at 12:13...I just want to make sure you are getting my messages. Message deleted...Fourth message...received today at 1:46pm. Ari, page me when you get this message. I need to get your perspective on some things. Plus, I just need to hear your voice. We haven't had a chance to talk in a while and...I really miss you. You know the number."

Hmmmmmmmmm. Now, I'm going to address this in an orderly fashion. First of all, I would think that Trey would know better than to call me at all anymore. It's not like I have returned any of his phone calls lately. Plus, the fact that I haven't gone over to his place in forever should serve as a major clue to my lack of interest in him. He can't come over to mine because I never told him where I lived.

Single girls' rule #6: Never tell a man where you live until you feel like it is ok with you if he just drops by. Otherwise, you will be faced with all sorts of crazy scenarios surrounding some man who has been axed from your phone list sitting outside your crib writing down how many times he saw your lights come on.

Really, Trey needs to stop begging. This is really getting ridiculous. At first, I thought the shit was a trip. Something of an ego boost for me. Then, a little later in the game, it became funny; something for me and my crew to laugh about over a pitcher of margaritas and some quesadillas. But now, I'm starting to get annoyed with Trey. I thought avoidance would do the trick; but, apparently I was SO WRONG! The fact that he is cheap doesn't help his case one bit, either. I would at least hesitate over giving him the boot if he was giving a sistah a decent gift every now and again. *A sundae? From McDonald's? That you won?* Please tell me that he is playing. But, some lonely sistah somewhere in the world would probably love to lick the nuts off his free sundae; it just ain't me.

Now that I've given Trent his 5 minutes of fame, I will devote my attention to the last caller. My emotions are mixed up on this one. I will start by giving you something that he didn't...his name: Hunter. Now, you may remember me mentioning him to you in the beginning of things. But, I haven't exactly spoken to him in a while. Hunter is

70

inaccessible to me most times; and unavailable others. He usually tries to squeeze me into his schedule just enough to insure that I don't take his name off of my list. At first, this used to annoy me quite a bit. But eventually, I learned to play the game by the rules that he made up. It has probably been about 5 months since I have hooked up with Hunter. So, I'm sure that he is just trying to test the waters for a maintenance call.

We met at the local bistro that I frequent whenever I am in one of my artsy moods. They sell good wine, pastries and pretty much anything else that your heart would desire up in that joint. They also have tables set for your lounging pleasure; as well as different cooking classes and wine tastings that they hold on a bi-monthly basis. Well, about a year and a half ago, I signed up to take a class entitled: "The Sensual Art of Bread Making". Now, I will be the first one to tell you that the title, alone, did wonders for me! The freak within me was crying out to know what was so sensual about making bread. So, I signed up, paid my fee and showed up a week later to begin my journey for the next 4 weeks; two days a week. I figured that I would at least learn some impressive skill by taking the class; or, I would gain 10 pounds eating all the new bread that I would make.

The day of the first class was one of the worst rain storms in history. I started to skip out on class. But, I decided against it due to the fact that it was the first day and all. The class was being held in a traditional looking cooking room in the back of the bistro. When I arrived, I was about ten minutes late; due to trying to find a decent parking space that wouldn't leave me totally drenched. So, I entered the room and slid onto a stool about two-thirds of the way in the back of the room. After I got myself adjusted and started honing in on the particulars that we would need for the class, I noticed the most stunning man was leading the discussion. I blinked in fear that I was having some sort of out-of-body experience. However, that was not the case. I pulled out my compact and made sure that I at least looked good for someone who had just stepped in out of the rain.

When I finished approving of my appearance, I sat up as straight as I could and gave the instructor my undivided attention. At least, that is, after I finished assessing the demographics of the class. The instructor informed us that we would be taking a field trip around the bistro in order to get our supplies that we needed for the class and for doing so, we would receive a 15% discount of our entire purchase.

So, after about twenty more minutes of instruction, we were released into the store to search for our supplies. I had wandered over to the deli to try out some of the samples that they had on display. I was admiring the display of cheese and decided to try out a couple of cubes to kill my curiosity, as well as my hunger pangs, when I felt a hand on my shoulder. I turned around to face the instructor of our course.

"Hi there. I see that you are getting your daily requirement of calcium today. How about letting me serve you?" asked the caramel-colored man standing before me with a piece of mesquite-smoked Monterey Jack cheese between his fingers.

"Hello yourself. I'm feeling liberated enough to oblige your request. By the way, my name is Ari. A student of your culinary class," I smiled flirtatiously.

"Ari…what an intriguing name! Your beauty overwhelmed my good judgment and manners. My name is Hunter. Hunter Morgan."

And with that, Hunter took the cheese that he was holding and placed it against my parted lips. I eagerly lapped at the cheese as though it were melted; hot to the touch. As I chewed, Hunter went on to tell me about which cheeses to use with certain wines. I never knew cheese could be so interesting! Better yet, I never knew that talking about cheese could make my panties wet! All of a sudden, I had the intense urge to reenact the scene in "Don't Be a Menace to South Central While Drinking Your Juice in the Hood" and have him pour melted cheese all over my naked body. OK. I know that I am tripping a little bit. But, he had my mind on other things besides the cheese.

Anyway, we talked for about five additional minutes before he moved further into the bistro to help others gather their supplies. Needless to say, my attention span was shot for the remainder of the evening. I was feeling the heat pretty badly. So, I figured that I would just hang around a few extra minutes after class and see if I could entice the teacher into a "taste" test of my own. There were a few stragglers that remained once we finished. So, I took my time gathering my things and waited them out. Once the last person exited, I asked Hunter a question.

"Hunter, do you think that it would be possible to bundle up a few cheese squares, grab the appropriate bottle of wine and chill for a little bit. I feel restless and not quite up to going home yet."

Hunter smiled and said, "I think that can be arranged. I'm not into being foolish; and I think it would be foolish of me to turn down the request of a woman of such remarkable beauty. I would be delighted to join you."

Now, I know that I moved a bit quickly on this one. For one, I knew that I was not ready to invite this strange man into my home. It wasn't because I felt threatened or in fear of my safety; but, you have to wait and get to know a person's tendencies before you allow them to come into your space. So, since I made the first move, and he took the bait, I was going to have to come up with an alternative. I waited while he gathered his material and we walked into the bistro to pick up some cheese and a bottle of wine (complete with glasses) to go. Then, I followed him outside to put his things away in his car. After he finished, I told him that I felt like going for a drive and asked him along for the ride.

I was driving my midnight blue Suburban and I had come up with a little plan. I drove over to Cinnamon Park and parked by the man-made lake area so that we could experience some scenery while we talked and got better acquainted. We talked, nonstop, for almost an hour. I learned quite a bit about Hunter; including the fact that he was married. I was at least thankful that he disclosed that information to me right off the bat because I would hate to find out later by way of some mad woman stalker chick giving me the blues. Anyway, Hunter told me that he was an architect for a small engineering firm in town; and that he had several passions, specifically anything he could do with his hands. At this point, whether he knew it or not, I was extremely turned on. #1. A Fine Man. #2. A Man Who Is Good With His Hands. OH MY!!

"I must admit that I find myself feeling a rather strong attraction to you even though we just met. I hope that I'm not being too forward," Hunter said uneasily.

I smiled, wantonly, at his statement; or should I say, his understatement. But before I could speak, his next statement caught me completely off guard.

"I would like to see you again. I'd like to see where this can go. I'm a realist with no expectations for the future. But, I feel that I would be foolish to walk away from this moment..." And with that, he leaned in to me and planted the most tender kiss on my nose, first; then my chin.

I was paralyzed with wanting for this man. I wanted to meet his advance with the return of intense passion. I became overwhelmed by the heat below and moved forward to give him a reason to rethink all of his life decisions. As I leaned into him, I was met by the index finger of his right hand to my lips.

"I want us to stop before we go any further. Please accept my invitation to visit me at my studio on Wednesday of next week. We can be alone and have some uninterrupted time with one another. Please say yes," Hunter pleaded.

So, I did; and we agreed to meet the following week. My days were really starting to look up because I was going to get the opportunity to see this gorgeous creature three days in the coming week. So, my anticipation ran off the charts. I don't know what it was about him; but Hunter had "it". You know the thing that sets a man apart from every other Joe Blow you meet. It goes beyond charisma. It definitely goes well beyond looks and good breeding. He was stimulating. That's the only excuse that I can give for not walking away from the whole thing once he told me about his marriage.

So, I will fast forward to our meeting on Wednesday (because cooking classes were a blur since I was not paying all that much attention to the lesson). He gave me the address to a loft in the arts district; which is about 15 minutes away from the bistro location. I dressed warmly because the temperature had dropped from my beloved 80's to an uncomfortable 42 degrees. I arrived at his studio about 8:15pm, went into the lobby to buzz his loft and awaited his acceptance. While I waited, I couldn't help but wonder what I was really doing. I must say that I did not have the most innocent of intentions. Just looking at him made me want to commit all sorts of sins; not just stopping short with fornication and adultery, alone. I heard the beep and I pulled the gate up and got into the private elevator headed for #11. When I got to Hunter's floor, he greeted me at the elevator with a warm hug and a welcoming smile.

"I'm glad that you could make it, Ari. I was just about to prepare the dough for the parmesan dinner rolls. Perhaps you could assist me with that?" Hunter questioned.

"Sure, I figured you may take the day off from cooking. I know it must feel like work since you are required to do it at least twice a week to help the disabled," I quipped.

"Actually, cooking is quite therapeutic for me. It's much less hectic than my day job. Plus, don't you think a man should have a penchant for cooking; especially if he loves to...eat?" Hunter asked seductively.

At that moment, I glanced at the ring finger of his left hand and noticed the vacancy. Maybe he did that for cooking purposes. Maybe that is a sign of some sort. Maybe, I'm just looking for an excuse to run from this temptation.

Hunter took my jacket and showed me into the kitchen where everything was on display. I washed my hands and reached for the bowl with the dough inside. Now, I'm no stranger to the kitchen, mind you; however, I am no Mrs. Baird's either. Apparently, Hunter noticed my lack of ease in the bread department and decided to help me out.

"Put your hands at the bottom of the bowl and grab at the dough from the bottom. Like this." Hunter said and proceeded to stand behind me to position himself.

He stood behind me and interlaced our fingers so that he could show me how it's done. Suddenly, I became aware of his nearness to me. I could feel his breath in my hair. I could smell the Dunhill Eccentric exuding from his chest. I could feel his muscles working inside of his chenille sweater. I also felt his manhood rising against my flesh. But, even with all that, he didn't stop kneading. Neither did I. I felt myself fall against his chest and give in to his rhythm. I wanted to face him at that moment and give him the most passionate kiss that I could muster. But, he wouldn't let me turn around. Instead, he pressed his body into mine; with his face in my hair for several minutes. Then, he lifted my hair off my neck and began to nuzzle me from behind. I could feel his every inhalation. I reached behind me and began to massage his yearning. I felt his heartbeat quicken as he gave in to his desire. At this point, he spun me around to face him. I could see the fire in his eyes for me. He knew that I saw it and returned his flames. He picked me up and placed me onto the island area. I fell backwards onto the awaiting area and he lifted my skirt. I heard fabric rip as he tore my panties from my body and released me from my prison. He buried his face into my love and I begin to sing hymns and chant exaltations. After my body gave into his demands, Hunter came face-to-face with me; allowing me to taste my own heat. I did so; sucking at his lips and chin like a woman carnally possessed.

"Ooooooooohhh…It's been so long since I've felt like this. You taste so good. I need to feel you," Hunter panted.

With that, I let him meet his needs and allowed him to surpass my expectations. I felt so good that I didn't want the feeling to end. I felt like a champion who had won the grand prize.

That is, until his cell phone rang an hour later and the conversation confirmed that I had nothing to show; but my indiscretions.

CHAPTER 10: SIMEON

"Daddy? Can I have a remote control Hummer for Christmas?" Casey questioned me as she looked at the picture in the Wal-Mart sales paper.

I sighed and said, "This is July, Casey. You still have half a year to go until Christmas."

I swear that girl asks for everything that they make in that store! I need to go down there today and pick up some more supplies for my tackle box for my fishing expedition this weekend. But, that is out of the question with Casey at my side. I know that there is no such thing as peace and tranquility in the parental world; but, Ms. Casey will not be making that trip! I'll let her mother deal with her.

I cannot wait to go fishing. I tried to convince Trent to go on the trip with me and the fellas. But, that should have been named "mission impossible" because Trent is not the fisherman type. The only thing that he is interested in catching is some unsuspecting victim; I mean, woman who hasn't heard about his trifling ways!

I'm so excited about this trip because it feels as though it has been years since I have had the chance to go away with the guys for the weekend and enjoy the great outdoors. My friend Cashon is supplying his boat for the trip. It has an upper and lower deck to accommodate those who are fishing and those who want to relax on the inside. We plan on leaving at the crack of dawn on Friday morning and coming back on Sunday afternoon.

David, Carl and Moteif are coming on the trip, also. I haven't seen Moteif since college. David and I work together in the delivery industry; while Carl runs a chain of automotive supply parts stores in the area.

Of all of us, Motief is considered to be the eclectic one of the group. I would consider him to be a free spirit in many ways. He had plenty of opportunities to show this side of himself in school. Moteif was one vocal cat. It used to be a lot of fun watching him pick up one cause after another and champion it until its death; or, until he lost interest in it. After college, he took off to Australia and became a licensed pilot. He flew tourists around for donations and lived in a houseboat along the shore side. He did that for awhile; and then, he moved to New York and started a petition to move the Statue of Liberty; or some other cause just as ludicrous.

I probably forgot to mention that Moteif was not only strange by some standards; but, he was an extremely gifted artist. I have to admit that I rode the coattails of his artistic abilities in college quite a bit. It wasn't that I couldn't pull the ladies all by myself; because I could. It was the type of women who were drawn to men of his talents that I was interested in.

For example, our junior year in college, Moteif posted flyers around campus, and in town, to recruit female models for a piece that he was going to enter into a national art contest. We requested photos to be mailed to us prior to being contacted for a possible interview. Needless to say, everybody wanted to be a star! So, there were countless messages from women in the area that wanted to arrange a sitting. Moteif had me act as his agent. So, we set up a screening for about 30 women to come by and audition for us in the basement of the Art Department; which Moteif had a key to for after hours usage.

We took two evenings and interviewed 15 women on two consecutive days. Off the bat, I explained to them that it was a nude portrait that he would be painting. We even had a waiver for them to sign stating the particulars of the "interview". I couldn't believe what women were willing to do for some national coverage! Needless to say, I had a good time!

Once we looked everyone over to make sure that they didn't have any stab wounds, pot holes, bullet wounds or massive amounts of scar tissue, we finally narrowed it down to three females: Karen,

Nandra and Lorielle. All three of them were banging! Nandra was a sophomore at another university across town. Karen was the niece of one of the ladies who worked in the Café at the Student Union. Kind of strange, huh? Lorielle worked at Foley's in the mall across town. I am still amazed at how far the news traveled of our little artistic venture.

Well, the short of this story is that we threw a little party for the ladies at one of my boy's cribs off campus to show our appreciation to them before we made the final selections. This gave me a chance to work my magic on a smaller, more intimate level. I didn't really have a preference for one lady over the other. I wanted Lady Luck to embrace me with her good fortune and give me at least one of 'em. They were all too fine to pass up! Plus, at least one of them had a job that I knew of!

Anyway, the soirée was set for 10:00pm at my boy John's house. I had already come through earlier to ensure that the place was clean and that it looked like a den for romance. John was out of town with the basketball team; so, no interruptions from his end. Everything was all set. Motief and I were both in place when the ladies showed up around 10:35pm. We were sipping on drinks and feeling the groove of the music when Motief began thanking everyone for participating and being down with the cause. He told the ladies that he still hadn't made his final decision on who to choose for the portrait; but, he had a game in mind that would certainly help to influence his decision.

At this point, Nandra rolled her eyes, heavenward, and lamented, "It figures. If all you want to do is see who is good at what; then we could have got our thang on already!"

Hood rat! I thought silently. That helped me to cross her name off of my list of potential sex partners for the future. I had a feeling Moteif was up to something way more clever than that. It was a feeling I had; not that he had let me in on his little scheme.

Moteif spoke up. "No, that's not quite what I had in mind. But, if the mood changes, we are all consenting adults. Do what you feel."

Nandra calmed down long enough to let the man finish introducing the next act in his play.

"I was hoping that I would be able to see more than just your bodies; as beautiful as they are. I was counting on getting a peek at your minds. Could I engage everyone in a friendly game of Taboo? Men against the women." Moteif said.

Now, I must admit my mental state had not quite caught the grasp of what Moteif was up to at this point. But, I shrugged my shoulders and went along with the program. To make a long story short, we teamed up and the women beat the pants off of us, literally. We switched it up to make it a little more interesting by having whoever lost a round to remove an article of clothing. Unfortunately, we didn't plan on losing; so, it defeated our purpose. But, we had fun.

The night ended and everyone went their separate ways. Life went on; as usual. Moteif painted a stunning portrait of all three women blended into the head of an orchid in full bloom. This naturally impressed all three of the ladies; and they all started seeing him on a personal level. Strange, huh? Each one knew about the other one; yet they continued to see him individually, as well as collectively. See? That's what I'm talking about! That's why he is my boy!

Hopefully during this trip, he and I will be able to catch up on what's been going on lately. Who knows? Maybe, he will have a new story to tell me!

I pulled up to Cashon's around 5:27am. I was closely followed by Carl; and then Moteif sidled up. David was already inside the garage with Cashon polishing the front end of his boat.

"What's up fellas?" I asked everyone as I approached the house.

"Nothing much. Are you gentlemen ready for some reel action?" questioned Cashon as he put the finishing touches on his prized possession.

Carl replied, "I was born ready, my man. I'm like a fish out of water on land. Just show me the lake!"

"Moteif, my man. What has it been? 8 or 10 years? What has my brotha been up to lately?" David asked.

Moteif smiled; flashing us with his Caribbean pearls. "It has been far too long for all of us. I've been in South Carolina on business for the last few months. But, we have plenty of time to catch up on all of the details. It looks like we are all here now. When will we be ready to ride out? I can't wait to get this show on the road!"

David joked, "I don't know why you tryin' to rush somebody. It ain't like you gonna catch anything bigger than a crawdad anyway."

More laughter and jokes were shared among us as we all loaded up our equipment and got into the truck. Cashon went back inside to the Mrs., gave his goodbyes and we were off and running.

I claimed the back seat so that I could stretch out, undisturbed. David and Carl got into the seat in front of me; while Moteif rode up front with Cashon.

"I've got a new CD that we can ride to," Carl offered.

"Naw, man. For right now, we are going to make good use of this satellite radio that I'm paying for. It's got any type of music that you want to hear. Plus, I don't need for ya'll to start relaxing and going to sleep on the drive down. We have plenty of time to rest and relax while we're down there. I know that you all are used to getting up early. All of you got jobs, right Moteif?"

"Oh, so now who's Mr. Fucking Funny Man of the group? You know that I have always had my own thing going. I'm just not as traditional as the rest of you cats," Moteif replied.

"I know. I get bored with the traditional thing myself," added Carl. "Sometimes I feel like I'm going to scream if I keep up this routine. Simeon has it better than me. At least at the end of his shift, he can go home to Kia. She really has done a good job of keeping herself together. Good looking out, Simeon!"

I smirked as I punched Carl in his back. "Don't get yourself hurt! Don't worry about what Kia is looking like. You need to keep your focus on Julie."

"OUCH!" Carl screamed as he rubbed the spot where I smacked him. "I was just giving you props on your wife. Julie hasn't been on her game lately. I figured she could learn a thing or two from your wife."

"Ya'll are a trip. Carl you know better than to be thinking about Kia, anyway. Simeon will whoop your ass for less," Cashon teased.

"I know you not starting in on me, Cashon. Your wife has been looking hot lately, too. Neither one of you best not be caught slipping; or I'm on it!" Carl roared. "You got a woman, Moteif?"

"Yeah, your momma said to tell you to behave yourself on this trip right before I left this morning," Moteif cracked. "Oh yeah, and your sister said what's up when I left her crib the night before!"

With all of the cracking going on, we were hard pressed to hear the sirens and notice the flashing red lights that were behind us.

"Shit, I know they're not coming for me!" Cashon exclaimed as he looked out of his rearview mirror at the cop in pursuit of him.

Cashon slowed, pulled over and popped open his glove compartment to get out his registration. Now, Cashon's truck has tinted windows; so, it made it even more difficult to see with it still being dark outside since it was around 6:15 in the morning. Cashon looked out of his window to address the officer approaching the vehicle. He noticed that he was taking his time checking out the license plate and shining his flashlight; making it was hard to see him.

"I can't believe this! I wasn't speeding was I? It doesn't matter. Ya'll just stay cool and I will handle this," Cashon sighed worriedly.

At that moment, the officer tapped on the glass. When Cashon rolled down the window, the most beautiful black creature in a uniform appeared before us.

"License and registration, please," Officer Beauty said.

Cashon questioned the Officer. "Officer, I don't understand what I did wrong. I was going the speed limit."

"I understand. Just a moment," Beauty said; and with that, she walked back to her patrol car to run Cashon's driver's license. After what felt like an eternity, Officer Beauty came back to the truck and shined her light on all of us.

She spoke, "I need to see identification from all of you."

We all fished out our wallets and handed our ID's to Cashon. I could tell that he was getting frustrated; but, he was still trying to maintain his cool.

"Officer, could you please tell me what this is all about? We are on our way to a fishing expedition and are not trying to cause any trouble. What is this all about?" he continued.

"One moment sir and I can answer all of your questions. Please, just sit tight and I will be right back," Officer Beauty replied and went back to her squad car with the remainder of our ID's.

"I hope none of ya'll got any warrants," I whispered. "If so, it's gonna be a long weekend." I was trying to make light of the situation because I really didn't want this deal to put a dark cloud over our trip.

After another eternity passed, Officer Beauty came back to the truck.

"I'm sorry gentlemen. We are looking for a murder suspect that is believed to be traveling in this area. I didn't mean to alarm you; I just needed to make sure that he hasn't stowed away in anyone's vehicle. I am stopping all cars that come along this area until the manhunt ceases. You gentlemen enjoy your trip."

With that, Officer Beauty went back to her squad car, made a u-turn and went back in the direction from which she had come.

"Murder suspect?" Carl piped up. "It's really getting crazy around here."

"Yeah. I hate that we met her as suspects. I would have loved to have gotten her phone number," chimed David.

I was in a trance at this point. Here I am all ready to enjoy some peace and fish grease and somebody has up and killed somebody! There are just some things that you just can't be prepared for.

Oh well, I hope they find the killer.

CHAPTER 11: MAINE

"Hey man, I need to know what time your plane lands this evening. I've got tickets to that play that's in town starring Toni Braxton down at the Amphitheatre," Julius said.

"No can do man. I told you that I promised Ari that I would go over some of her sketch work for the Henderson project later on tonight. That thing has my reputation riding on it and it has to be perfect. Sorry man," I told him.

Relentless, Julius continued, "I can't believe you gone let me down like that. This is Toni Braxton that we're talking about! You know she split up with her husband; so, that leaves the door wide open for me as his replacement."

"Naw man, you go on ahead. I'm sure you can find someone to take in my place. How about one of your friend girls that you always seem to have on stand by?" I asked.

Julius retorted, "No. This play is gonna be playa's paradise! Once all of those women come out of the show during intermission all angry and disgruntled; I plan to be standing around during intermission getting my scope on. I figured the two of us could work the house over."

"Well, let me know how everything went down. You still shooting ball this weekend? You know Terrence got some new kids on his crew that could use a lesson or two."

Julius responded, "Yeah, I'll be through there around warm-up time. I'll holla back at you and let you know what you missed. I might let you have one of my reserves."

I laughed and said, "Whatever, I'll holla at you when I get back."

I have one more piece of business to attend to before I board the plane this evening. I have been here for the last four days trying to make sure that everything was going according to plan. As far as I see it, some heads are gonna roll from what I've discovered; and I don't plan on being on the chopping block.

First, I have to give you a little background on the situation at hand. Cyril Connors is the head of the warehouse in Monterey where the distribution center is housed. Cellcast, Inc. has strong ties to the distribution deal in Monterey that go much farther than basic sales and logistics can possibly account for. When I was pursuing a promotion into the executive world of Cellcast, a man by the name of Tony Sargosa took me under his wing and vowed to lead me to the Promised Land. Of course, I had the usual visions of dollar signs that dance in the heads of those who live paycheck-to-paycheck; so, I was more than happy to take Tony up on his offer. He seemed to be well connected within the company and he had the respect of most of the people I had come into contact with during my time there.

I felt really good about the chance to get to work so closely with him. For one, he sought me out personally; which helped my ego achieve new heights. Secondly, the fact that he was the Vice-President of Financial Affairs did nothing but help matters even more. I had only been with Cellcast, Inc. for about five years; and had spent about two of those years in the Young Executive's Program. This program was designed as a career fast track to identify those who wanted to pursue careers within the company on a senior management level.

One day, I got a voicemail from Tony requesting my presence in his office for a meeting. I was shocked because I could not imagine what he could want to talk to me about. I was also scared to death that this could mean that I had messed up in a major way and was about to receive my walking papers. I reported to his office, as he requested, and waited until his assistant gave me the go ahead to go through those cherry wood doors that led to his office. As I waited, I couldn't help but think that with hard work and determination, I too could be a part of this world. I was willing to dedicate myself to doing whatever it took to make it.

So, when I received my summons, I went into Tony's office to accept my fate. It turned out that Tony was one of the mentors in the Young Exec's Program and wanted to know how I felt about being his protégé. Without any hesitation, I readily accepted his offer and we talked for about an hour (kind of a getting to know each other better session). Anyway, when I left Tony's office, I was on cloud nine. I couldn't believe that I had just hit the career lottery like that!

Our relationship progressed over the years and; just as he promised, Tony pulled some strings to land me a gig as the Assistant Vice-President of Distribution and Sales in the Southern Region of the United States! The job came with a hefty paycheck; but, it also came with many other strings attached to it, as well. There was a reorganization that took place shortly after I received my promotion that landed Tony in the VP seat of Distribution and Sales, now making him by direct supervisor.

I went to an advisory council meeting and was briefed on the particulars of my role within the company. At this time, Tony told me about the layout of the Southern region and how I was to travel back and forth to several of our distribution sites, with Monterey as the main focus, and monitor the processes of each site. That is where meeting Cyril Connors came into the picture.

On my first trip to Monterey, Tony and I met with Cyril at the distribution center to discuss my coming on board and how we would be handling our affairs from that point forward. I was expecting notes and agendas to be passed among us so that we would all be on the same page regarding our roles and responsibilities. What I actually got was a cigar in my hand and a pat on my back as we took a tour of the facilities.

"Let me introduce you to the Second Line Manager: Rosito Morris," Cyril said as he waved to a stocky Hispanic male in one of the front offices.

"Rosito, I want you to meet Maine Richards. He will be coming down to check on our little operation from time to time from the district office," Cyril explained to the man.

Rosito stood and extended his hand. "It's good to meet you, boss man. I hope you stick around longer than the last guy. I guess he didn't have a stomach for the business," he sneered.

What the hell is he talking about? I wondered silently as I shook his hand.

We continued our tour of the plant and made the rounds visiting with various people; while dispensing with introductions. I got a chance to see most of the operations; with the exception of the assembly line and packing center. Cyril said that they were under construction and were a "hard hat only" zone until modifications were complete. Tony and I went to lunch with Cyril so that they could catch up on some business matters. I was just along for the ride. That is, until I caught a part of their conversation that sounded suspicious.

"The government inspectors have been coming around over the last few months wanting to perform an audit of our packing process. I told them that it would only interfere with our line and slow our production down. Our line is up to code. That's all that they need to be concerned with," remarked Cyril angrily.

"I thought that you had a contact over in their division that was supposed to quell their riot?" Tony quizzed. "This shit would not be happening if you would handle your business like I told you."

Cyril thought for a moment. Then he replied, "Tony, this has nothing to do with my contact not being on board with the program. This thing is getting bigger than us. It's like a fucking virus. They didn't even come from Carlos' division. I think you need to check your facts. Somebody's talking."

We finished our meal, as well as our business, and headed back to the district office by nightfall. I had had a lot of information to absorb for my first few days on the job; and I was in desperate need of an outlet. But, this was not to happen just yet.

By the time that we got back into the office, I had a message to call Cyril as soon as I got in. *What could this be about?* I knew that we had just left the facility and I hadn't been in the game long enough to start receiving urgent phone calls from the play makers. I went into my office and dialed the number that was listed on the message from Cyril. The phone rang at least six times before someone picked it up.

However, the voice on the other end didn't sound like the man that I had just met earlier today. He spoke in a gruff, distorted voice and said: "College boy, you are in way over your head. Back away from this thing while you still have your legs!"

Then the phone went dead.

CHAPTER 12: PHYLLIS

Today is not a good day for me. This is the morning after; and my conscious is really kicking a whole in my head. I called my Prayer Line Mentor Donna this morning to see if she could help pull me through.

"Donna, I'm sorry to be calling you so extra early this morning. I know that we are about to go online in about thirty minutes; but, I have something I really need your help on this morning."

Donna yawned audibly, "Girl, you know if it wasn't for the Lord's work, I would cuss your ass out, now don't you? What is it that can't wait until God's people are up and functioning?"

I hesitated. I know that I have already started the forward motion on this thing. I just hope that she won't trip too hard on me for what I'm about to tell her.

"What is it, girl? You have come this far. Always remember, there is nothing too hard for God," Donna coaxed.

I started in, "Well, you remember when I told you about me swearing off sex until I got my act together? You know that I have had some problems trying to keep it together; my legs, I mean," I stammered. I was still second-guessing my decision to tell Donna. But, here goes nothing.

"Well?" Donna questioned. "It couldn't be worse than some of the stuff you've already done; not that I'm judging you. So, what is it?"
"I was watching T.V. at home last night, minding my own business, when I came across one of those real sex shows that they have on HBO," I said.

Donna laughed, "Ain't nothing wrong with watching T.V., Phyllis. You better not have me up before the crack of dawn for no T.V. nonsense."

"Well, I was up watching this show and they really had some freaky stuff going on. Men on men, women on other women, everybody on everybody else. I have to say that the whole thing was getting to me. But, I couldn't change the channel. I tried to turn it and act like I never saw it; but that didn't work," I continued.

"Okay? Then what?" Donna demanded to know. At this point, I could tell that she was running out of patience with me. At this point, I had run out of patience with myself.

"So, I went down to the pool hall. You know the one on the corner next to that car dealership?" I asked.

"You talking about the one that Jarrod goes to all the time. The one where most of the people from the packing plant hang out after their shift? What were you doing up there? What time was it when you went in? You know that it is not safe to be wandering the streets at strange hours of the night, anyway!" Donna admonished me.

"Yeah. It's the same hall that they all go to after they finish working. It was over halfway full when I got there just after midnight. I know that it wasn't safe for me to be out like that. But, I figured that I needed to get out and get my mind off of sex and I knew that I could be around some familiar faces while I was working my frustration out on the pool table."

"Uh huh," Donna added.

"Well, I went in and started talking noise with Bim, the Foreman for the night crew. You know how he is when he gets to talking shit. So, we played a few games of pool; and then, I got the idea that we should play for money since we were even in score. I figured that I could come up and go on that shoe shopping spree that I told you about last month that I was planning and…"

"Okay, Phyllis. I got all that. Now get to the part that's got you calling me so early. You can skip the extra details, alright?" Donna stated impatiently. I forgot that she can be short with a sistah when she hasn't had her coffee and oatmeal in the mornings.

"So, anyway. Bim, Michael and Frank all said that they wanted to play me for cash. I was cool with it because I really am a closet pool shark. You remember when my daddy used to run numbers for Domino? Well, I learned to play pool from some of the best hustlers out there. So, I racked and played Michael for 4 games at $100 a game; which I was three up on. Next, it was Frank's turn. I whooped up on Frank for all 4 games! So, with $700 in my pocket, I knew that I couldn't go wrong. By the time I finished putting a hurting on Frank, it was almost 2:00am. Bim started saying that he needed to go home before his wife started tripping; and would I mind if he let a substitute play in his place. I didn't care who played because I was whooping ass and taking names; and so far, I had three names already on my list. So, I waited about ten minutes while they tried to figure out who would play for Bim. Some new guy on their crew named Lovell said that he would take Bim's place; but, he wanted to change the stakes to really make the game interesting."

"Uh huh," Donna managed.

"Well, Lovell started saying that we were playing with weak odds; and that he would play me five games at $200 a game; with winner taking all in the end! So, I racked again, since I won all of the other sets, and we began to play.

Now, I have to tell you Donna, that Lovell was kinda fine. So, I realized that he was distracting me a little bit with his steel toe work boots and those work pants that were holding on to his thighs for dear life! Anyway, we played the first three games and I was up by two. I'm telling you Donna, this was my night! I should have bought a lottery ticket the night before because I couldn't have had any better luck than what I was having. I knew that I just needed one more game to put it in the bag for me. I had already picked out a nice pair of Anne Klein's that I was going to get at Neiman's when I got off work tomorrow. Anyway, Lovell started really talking noise and saying that I should quit while I was ahead; or I might regret it and how he didn't want to see me crying and everything. Now, at this time, most people had started clearing out of the hall. It was only me, Lovell, Frank, Michael, Stan and Meshell-you remember she's the dyke chick that works on the night shift with Jarrod 'nem?"

Donna exhaled, "Yeah, I know Meshell."

I kept going. "There were a few more people in front at the bar with Jarrod and the rest of them."

"See, that Jarrod keeps me on the Prayer Line. I have told him about all that staying out after work and drinking. See, that's why he never has any energy to do the things that I need for him to do around here!" Donna exclaimed angrily about her husband.

"Well," I continued, "with all of the noise going on, I lost the next game. So, I needed the last game to clean house. But, that's around the time that everything else turned ugly and Lady Luck left me stranded. I lost the last two games and I owed Lovell $1700!"

"What!" Donna screamed. "I know that you know better than to do some stupid shit like that! What the hell were you thinking Phyllis! This ain't even your pay week yet. How did you get that kind of money?"

"That's just it, Donna. I didn't have the money to bet with in the first place! I had no intention of losing. I couldn't believe that my luck had run out on me like that! I'm sorry, Donna! I know that you are disappointed in me; but, there's more," I stammered.

"More? Phyllis, if this call isn't coming in from the hospital recovery unit, you are lucky they let you walk out of there with all of your limbs intact!"

"Well, I want to say how sorry I am again," I said to Donna; hoping that she knew how much I really meant it.

"I got that part, Phyllis. Just keep talking."

"So, when the game was over, Lovell was looking for his money, right?" I asked.

"As any self-respecting hustler would be after a take," Donna retorted.

"So, I had to come clean and tell him that I really didn't have his money. Lovell was furious! He started calling me all kinds of names saying that I stole money from his boys and how he was gonna make me pay! I was so scared; I didn't know what to do. So, Lovell pushed me into the back room and made me open the cellar door. I begged him not to hurt me and that I would give him his money back. All of a sudden, his attitude changed and he told me that it was okay; that he had already thought of a way to get $1700 out of my ass!"

"I know I'm not hearing what I think I'm hearing!" shouted Donna.

"Well, once I opened the cellar door, Lovell pushed me inside and locked the door. It was real dark and scary down there; and I was too scared to cry out for help. Anyway, I heard voices just outside of the door. Then, Lovell opened the door and flicked a dim switch shedding a moderate amount of light into the room. There was a lot of stuff stored down there. A lot of bottles and crates and stuff. In the corner, there was a futon sofa bed with a few boxes stacked on top of it."

Donna interrupted, "If you are saying what I think you are about to say, then we need to call the police and have them do a kit on you, Phyllis. We won't let those bastards get away with doing something horrible like that to you! I don't care what you did to them!"

"Just let me finish telling you, Donna. This is already hard enough," I began to cry. I felt the weight of the whole situation coming down on me at one time.

"When Lovell opened the door and pushed his way inside, he was followed by Michael, Frank and Meshell. I heard him tell somebody to stand by the door and let them know if someone was coming. I felt my face go hot and I was starting to really panic at this point. Lovell then told me that neither he nor anyone else was going to hurt me; but, he wanted what I owed him. With those words, he spun me around with my back facing him, reached under my skirt and ripped my panties off onto the floor. He began stroking my heat with his index finger; while kissing me on the back of my neck. Then, Michael came and parted my lips with his tongue; while Meshell stripped out of her clothes and stood behind

Lovell, massaging my breasts. I know I should have been screaming for help; but, the only sounds coming from me were guttural moans of pleasure. I couldn't believe what was happening!"

"So, ya'll had an orgy down at the pool hall! I need to start praying for your ass right now. Dear Lord, please remove the sin from Phyllis' loins..." Donna began.

"That's not all that I wish that he would remove, Donna," I injected. "We all fell into a heap on the futon mattress: groping, licking and sucking on one another. I swear that shit felt so damned good! It felt like an oasis between my legs; I hadn't felt that way in so long! There were hands and tongues everywhere. There was so much going on; I couldn't tell who was doing what most of the time. The next thing I know, I was being put on top of Lovell for me to fuck him missionary style. Michael had his dick in my mouth and Meshell was sucking on my nipples. All of a sudden, I felt a third dick enter me from behind."

"I thought you told me that there were only two dicks in the room! Now you adding shit!" Donna cried out impatiently.

"Donna, I swear to you that I'm not adding incorrectly. I was so caught up in the moment...I was so wet and everybody felt so good; I was just going with the flow. I promise you that I didn't mean to fuck your husband, too! I swear I didn't!"

Then, I heard the phone disconnect.

CHAPTER 13: KIA

"Since Simeon is gone on his fishing trip this weekend, I was thinking of having a little get-together at the house with some of the girls," I told Janette; one of my customers and long-time friends at the shop. She was in my chair getting her hair done to go to the club later on that night.

Janette responded, "I think that's a great idea! You know that you throw some of the best parties around. Do you think we should hire a stripper? I know a couple of guys that take their clothes off all the time! We wouldn't even really have to pay them a fee. Just make sure they get plenty of dollars!"

I laughed. "Janette, that is not the type of party I'm talking about. Plus, it would be just my luck to have Simeon come back from his trip early and I got a whole bunch of naked men running all over the house! Uh-uh! You can have that party, yourself!"

"Hey, Kia! Just tell me what time to show up! What do you want me to bring?" asked my shop mate Colleen; who had obviously been eavesdropping on our conversation from the start.

You really need to bring me my booth rent, I thought silently.

"I will let you know if I really decide to have it. I was just thinking out loud" I told Colleen.

I really hate to be rude; but every since Colleen came into my shop two and a half months ago, she has not been timely in her booth rent payments. So how are you going to drop into my conversation, invite yourself to a party that I don't even know that I'm having yet and then ask me about what to bring! BRING ME MY MONEY, BITCH! That's what you do! Anyway, let me calm myself down. I plan on talking to her about that shit if she doesn't pay me by tomorrow. I try to let people handle their business without me having to stand over them constantly like children. Casey Marie is more than enough for me to keep up with on the daily. I don't need to add any more at this point. Especially not any that I don't have a social security number for.

"Come on Janette, let me put you under the dryer," I said as we went to the back of the shop.

"I hope I don't have to stay under there too long. You know that I hate the dryer! Can you come up with a new style for me that don't require me sitting under a heat lamp?" Janette joked.

"Yeah, but it also requires a razor cut and some lotion for your bald head! Now, quit clowning and sit down before I put you out of here with your head wet!"

Once I put Janette under the dryer, I went to the front to check my appointment book. It was now 7:30pm on Friday night, and my 7:00pm appointment was missing in action. I didn't have to look at the book to know who it was supposed to be. I already knew that Javonna was going to be late. It wasn't because she did the courteous thing by calling to let me know that she would be running behind for her appointment. It was because she never seemed to have a decent concept of time; other people's time, that is. So, while I waited on Queen Bee to come into my life and grace me with her nappiness, I called over to Ms. Martin's to check on Casey Marie.

"Hello?" Mr. Martin answered the phone.

"Hi Mr. Martin. How are you doing today? This is Kia. I was just calling to check on Casey. Is your wife around?"

"Good talking to you Kia. I'll get her," Mr. Martin replied.

"Hello Kia. Aren't you busy doing heads? You don't have to worry about Casey. She is helping me to sew a dress that I'm going to wear for Women's Day at the church next month. You know Ms. Martin got to be sharp when she step in the church;

especially on Women's Day!" Exclaimed Ms. Martin.

"Now, Ms. Martin, you know that you are always the sharpest knife in the drawer! Not even the pastor's wife can touch your outfits!" I encouraged her.

Ms. Martin giggled. "Thank you, honey. You are so precious! Now you know that I want you to do my hair for Women's Day. In fact, don't bother paying me for keeping Casey this week and we can call it even."

Ms. Martin is not only precious; but she is a natural born hustler as well!

"No problem, Ms. Martin. You know that I will take care of you. I need to ask a favor of you, as well. I am thinking about having some people over on tomorrow night. Would it be okay if Casey Marie spent the night with you?" I asked gingerly.

"Sure, if you want to, you can run by here tonight and bring her an overnight bag; and she can stay with me until Sunday. That way, you don't have to worry about having to get her ready. You can just focus on what you need to do for your little 'ole party," Ms. Martin explained.

"Well, thank you. I think I will take you up on that offer. Will you put Casey on the phone so that I can talk with her please?" I asked.

"Sure. Casey? Casey? Telephone!"

"Hello?" Casey Marie answered.

"Hey baby, it's your Mama. I just wanted to let you know that you are going to spend tonight and tomorrow night with Ms. Martin. I'm gonna come through a little later tonight and bring a bag with your clothes in it for you."

"OK, Mama. Could you put my purple Kim Possible shirt and my jeans in there? And, could you put my Bratz dolls in the bag, too? I want to show Ms. Martin some of the clothes that I want her to make me!" Casey shouted excitedly.

"Now Casey, don't be over there showing out! And, don't give Ms. Martin any trouble. If I find out that you did, she is going to spank your butt and so will I!" I reminded my daughter.

"OK, Mama."

"It's yes ma'am," I prompted her.

"Yes ma'am," she repeated.

"So, I'll see you later on tonight when I come to drop the bag off. Be good and Mama will see you later."

"Bye, Mama!" Casey said. Then she hung up before I could say anything further.

I put the phone back down on the charger and started staring into space for a minute. Now, I really could throw a little shindig for me and my girls; and I didn't even have to sweat about what to do with Ms. Casey. This is so perfect! I need to chill and have me a little fun for a change. I seem to always be the one minus all the fun around here. Well, not entirely. But, I am going to make up for the little bit that I have missed!

So many details. *What do I want to have? Who all do I want to invite? What kind of music do I need to have?* Details! I will get it together tonight after I drop Casey's bag off. I need to stop by the mall tomorrow and get myself a new outfit. Better yet, I can do that now because it is now 7:52pm and still no Javonna!

I walked back to the back of the shop and tapped on the hood of Janette's dryer because she was asleep.

"Come on, Janette. Let me finish blow drying you so that I can get out of here. I got a party to plan for tomorrow night."

Rubbing the sleep out of her eyes, Janette smiled and said, "Now see, that's what I'm talking about! What time do I need to be there, girl? You sure you still don't need for me to get the strippers?" she questioned.

I smiled at her and said, "Naw, that's alright. It's not gonna be that kind of party. I'll call you later on tonight with all of the details."

CHAPTER 14: ARI

Sometimes you just don't have the creative energy to do what needs to be done. I have been staring at my sketch pad for the Henderson Project, off and on, for the last few days; and still nothing. I have been staring at the empty pages for the last 2 hours; ever since I got Simeon's page telling me that he would be returning to town tonight and that he wanted to look in on me and see what I had come up with. Boy is he going to be disappointed! I still have a few hours to kill before I'm held accountable for the work that I clearly haven't done. I need something that is going to get my creative juices flowing. I know! I will give my favorite masseuse a call. A good massage will definitely get rid of all that negative energy that's zapping my creativity. Let me get my cell phone.

"You have reached 'The Hands of Sampson'. I am unable to accept your call at the moment because I am on location in Barbados on an extended outcall. Please leave a detailed message and I will return the call soon. Thank you for calling 'The Hands of Sampson'...BEEP!"

I hung up. I felt tension that I didn't even know that I had creep into my neck and back muscles. Now what am I gonna do? I must admit that until now, I hadn't thought about doing what I just thought about doing. I still hadn't responded to Hunter's message. It has been a few months since we last saw one another. But now, I am in the middle of a full blown feeling of self-proclaimed weakness. I can't get a good massage, I am not working as efficiently as I need to on the Henderson Project and I haven't had sex like that since we last got together. I tried to forget about him since he obviously had other matters that he needed to attend to; like his wife or a divorce. But it is something about that man! He is just too damn fine! I can't believe that I managed to finish the culinary class and get my certificate in pastry and other fine food arts. There would be nothing wrong with calling him and checking to see how he was doing. No harm at all.

"You have reached the access line of Hunter Morgan. Please wait one moment while the system locates me," the system rang out.

"This is Hunter. How may I help you?" he answered.

I immediately felt warm. "Hello Hunter," I managed.

"A blast from the not-so-distant past. Ari Clayton, how have you been? I've missed you."

"I've been fine. Working. Busy. What has life been like for you lately?" I asked; dodging the mentioning of any feelings and avoiding his last statement.

"I haven't been as well as I could be. I must say. I saw a rainbow earlier and now you call. I think I may need to play the lottery because I have been smiled upon by the Gods today!" Hunter stated playfully.

I had to move quickly before I lost my nerve on the whole thing.

"Are you available for a few hours? I have some time and I wanted to know if we could meet for an early dinner or something."

"Hmmm...I can be free within the next 45 minutes to an hour. I just have to finish up some business with another client. We can meet back at my office in about an hour." He said.

Now, just for the record, I am not playing this thing by his rules. I called. I say where we meet. This meeting has to be on my terms for me to have any sort of leverage; which I feel is fading by each word that he speaks.

"How about we meet at the little sandwich shop on the corner of Jefferson and Hildegarde? I think that would give us a chance to catch up and grab a bite to eat at the same time."

Hunter audibly hesitated," Oh. OK. I can meet you there within the hour. You can go ahead and order that soup and sandwich combo that I like when you get there. I'll see you soon."

After we hung up the phone, I was still second-guessing my decision to call him. I wanted to see him. But, I know that it still may be too soon. But, I'm not going to be with him long enough to get myself into any trouble. I still have to meet Simeon when he gets in tonight to talk about the Henderson Project. That will definitely be my saving grace.

"I'm glad that you could make it on such short notice," I said as Hunter sat down in the chair across from me at the café. "I knew it was a shot in the dark. Thanks for coming."

Hunter smiled, "That's not a problem. You know that I would be hard-pressed to turn you down for anything. I must say. I am a little surprised by the fact that you called. You have obviously been keeping your distance from me lately. What's up? Did I get some communicable disease that I'm not aware that I have or something? Or, are you trying to break it off with a brother in a not-so-subtle way?"

It was my turn to smile. "It's just that I have been really busy lately. I haven't forgotten about you, though. That wasn't it at all. I have been focusing more on my priorities lately. I guess I felt like you were doing the same thing," I said with a little sting in my voice.

Hunter leaned back in his chair and looked at me for a moment.

"I know that you didn't like the way things were. But, I have been up front with you about all of that. You know that I'm in love with you, Ari. Things are just complicated right now. I just don't want to leave my kids hanging. If it weren't for them, I would have left years ago. You know that you really have my heart," Hunter said softly.

Now, I have to change the subject. I can't allow myself to be pulled into this emotional web of lust, lies, husbands and wives. But, I will admit that he looked damn good sitting here with me now.

"Look Hunter, I don't want to do this now. I just thought that we could sit and enjoy each other's company. I'm not trying to rehash the past; nor create a future. I promise you that I am fine with the way things are right now," I said.

Hunter bit into his sandwich, chewed and then sipped on his soup. *Damn his lips were full!*

"I see. Well, I want you to tell me just one thing and it will give me all the answers that I need from you," Hunter questioned me as he took my hand across the table and looked deeply into my eyes.

"What?" I smiled nervously. I was just trying not to begin perspiring as he held my hand in his firm, yet gentle grasp as he paused before asking his question.

"I want to know if you still want me? Have all of the feelings that you had for me abandoned you?"

Before I could answer him and let him know that he surpassed his question limit by asking two questions instead of one; Hunter kneeled down on the side of the table on one knee and began to stroke my face with his hand. As I looked at his eyes, I forgot about the fact that I was in a public place with a married man rubbing my face and putting his lips on mine. Now is not the time for losing good judgment.

As he pulled his lips from mine, he spoke, "Ari, I know that you still have feelings for me. Just give me a chance to work this thing out. I would like to have the opportunity to show you just how much I have missed you."

And with that, Hunter held up what resembled a hotel room key. Then, he reached for my hand and pulled me out of the café and onto the sidewalk outside.

"Hunter, I can't do this. Sex does nothing but confuse things between us. I can't go there with you again!" I exclaimed, trying to regain a modicum of composure.

Hunter turned, looked me in my eyes and took my face into the palms of his hands. His face drew closer and closer to mine; with his hands slowly massaging my neck, then my shoulders. I was beginning to feel the familiar throb of betrayal taking place between my legs.

Stop it! I tried to converse with my cootchie. *You can't react to any of this!*

"If you feel that sex confuses things for us, then…we don't have to have sex. Let me hold you and let you feel how my heart races in your presence," Hunter whispered into my ear as he pulled himself away from the kiss.

Well, if we aren't going to have sex; then I might be okay, my heart told my mind. I should be able to handle it. After all, I am a grown woman and I can say no to anything I damn well please! Right?

CHAPTER 15: SIMEON

I have to say that, so far, this trip has not quite been what I had imagined it to be. After we made it to the dock and got the boat in the water, it immediately began to pour down raining! But, Cason insisted that we go ahead and set sail because it may let up later and we could be the first ones to catch all of the fish that had let their guard down and would be circling near the top of the water. So, once we got the boat in the water and we were safely afloat, I went down to the lower deck to catch a quick nap. Now, don't get me wrong, I am used to rising early; but, I try to reverse the effects of a full-time job when I get my weekends. So, I settled in to one of the full beds onboard and began to dream for awhile.

When I woke up, I could tell that the day still looked somewhat dreary; even though the rain had let up, mostly. I could see the coastline through the window and it was so lush. I had not been to Mexico in a few years and I must admit that I was quite anxious to get out there and see what type of game their waters held. I know that we have all heard not to drink the water down there; which I still have no intention of doing. I just wanted to make the most of the trip. You know? I yawned and stretched as I stood to try to get my mind right for the day's activities. I could hear David, Carl and Moteif going at it up on the main deck.

"The only things that you are probably good at catching would be colds and venereal diseases," Carl howled. This brought immediate laughter from everyone.

"That's alright. You just make sure that your wife doesn't catch you with that pretty Puerto Rican girl that you hired to work as your assistant on the weekends! Who do you think that you are fooling? I know that you are hittin' that on the cool. You ain't slick, nigga!" David replied to Carl.

"Yeah, I know you just jealous because I got mine at home; plus, I can reel 'em in off the street! The last time you had a woman...Well. Come to think of it, I can't remember the last time!"

"Fuck you, Carl!" David shouted; obviously growing more annoyed with Carl's ribbing by the second.

Moteif spoke up. "Gentlemen. Gentlemen. Let's try and keep the peace. We have plenty of time for high-capping. How about we start casting our lines?

Cashon laughed, "See that's how I know ya'll ain't no real fisherman! The boat is still moving and you want to throw your line in the water! I have a little spot in mind that we're going to dock and set up. We'll wait until it clears up a little more and then we will continue south. From there, it will probably take us another hour to reach good waters. So, you girls have plenty of time to chill for now. I see Simeon has made it up from his beauty nap."

I smiled at all of them. They are all my boys; but, they are all a bunch of haters! I strolled over to the cooler and pulled out a Heineken to get my mood right. I popped the top and blew the clear fog from the opening before taking a drink. I went and stood next to Cashon near the wheel of the boat and looked into the distance.

"I'm really glad that we all got together to take this trip," I said letting the mist from the water and the rain hit my face.

Cashon sighed, "I know man. I couldn't wait to get away. I have had so much going on it's a trip. My job is tripping. My house note is too high. So is my blood pressure. I needed to get away and clear my head from all of the drama."

"Pressures like that can get to any man," I sympathized. "I am not too far from it myself. Casey Marie wants everything under the sun. Kia is high maintenance and getting higher by the year. The job is cool; but sometimes, you just want to break out of the mold. Do something different than what's expected of you, ya know?"

"Yeah. I know all about it. That's one of the reasons why I bought this boat. It's like my little piece of sanity. The one thing in my life that nobody else has any control over."

"Maybe that's what I need. A little something that's all mine. I thought I was getting that when I set up the game room with the big screen at the house; but, Kia has more parties and people over than I do!" I laughed at myself and how pitifully married I must've sounded to my boy. Just at that moment, David came up behind us waving a magazine.

"Say fellas. I've got just the thing to kick this trip into high gear. I hold in my hand the latest swimsuit edition of Booty Beauties Magazine for your viewing pleasures. Please feast your eyes on page 16; the second one on the left named Tania. Her mama and I used to go to school together back in the day. I wonder if I called her mama up and asked her for her number would she be down?" David wondered aloud.

"Man, you really are crazy…and desperate, I might add," I laughed. "You may want to give that up. Hell, if her mama looks half as good as she does;

you may stand a better chance of getting her number!"

Carl chimed in, "I would tell ya'll my two cents on the matter; but, D is so damn sensitive right about now that I don't want to have to whoop his ass during our little trip."

"Man, it's whatever! I'm about as sensitive as that rash you had on your balls a few months back. That's how sensitive I am!" David retorted as he walked towards the cooler for a beer.

"Nigga, don't play with me, here?" Carl started up again. "Truth be known, I ain't never really been fond of your ass, understand?"

All of a sudden, David rushed Carl with full force; knocking him backwards onto the boat floor. Carl screamed with surprise and proceeded to grab David by the neck and put him in a weird choke hold.

"I'm a kill you, nigga!" Carl yelled as David proceeded to whale on him. I rushed over and got David by the arms and yanked him off of Carl.

"Let me go, Simeon! Carl's been begging to get his ass kicked for a while. I'm about to hand him his ass on a platter," David huffed as he struggled to free himself.

Cashon yelled at us, "Ya'll need to get this shit under control! If something happens to my boat; there's gonna be extra ass whoopings all around!"

"Let that nigga go, Simeon. It's over," Carl coughed as though he were trying to catch his breath.

"Yeah, let me go Simeon," David said unconvincingly, "I already let him know what I'm about. He will keep my name out his mouth from now on I bet!"

About 5 seconds after I released David, Carl dove at his legs and knocked him off balance. Since Carl was still holding onto David; this sent the both of them over the edge and into the water.

"Oh shit!" I yelled. "Cashon, they fell off the boat!"

"I ought a turn this boat around and run over both of them! I told them to cut that shit out! See if you get the pole off the other side and try to fish 'em out."

By the time I went around to the other side and got the pole, I saw both David and Carl bob to the surface looking white as sheets.

"Man, get us out of here quick! There's a bag floating in the water with a hand hanging out of it," David screamed. "Hurry up!"

I know this nigga ain't trying to rush me after they started all this shit! But, I know I didn't just hear him say that he saw a bag floating with a hand in it? Did he? I know he can't be drunk yet because we've all had at least about a beer a piece! So, I stick the pole out to David first and pull him back towards the boat so that I can pull him up with my hand. Once I got him on board; then, I stuck the pole out to get Carl.

"Why don't you grab the bag and drag it with you?" I asked Carl as he waded in the choppy water trying to make his way closer to the boat.

"Naw man," Carl replied with chattering teeth, "It looks like it might be tied down to something. Plus, I ain't trying to play the part of no hero and get ate up out here! Black folks don't do well in no horror movies! Now, pull mc in!"

I pulled him onto the boat and went and got blankets for the both of them. It looked like they may have forgotten all about what landed them in the water in the first place because they were both sitting there looking like two lost souls.

"Man, what are we gonna do now?" Carl looked at me and asked; still shaking from the cold water and from what he had just seen in it.

I called for Moteif and Cashon to come over so that we could discuss what our next move should be.

"You know we need to call the Coast Guard or 911 or somebody," Cashon said worriedly.

Moteif nodded in agreement, "I know. But, if we do, they are going to have a lot of questions. It doesn't look good for a dead body to be anywhere near five black men."

Carl spoke, "Yeah man. I've been watching a lot of episodes of CSI: Miami. We should be okay calling the Coast Guard because they can look at the body and tell how long its been in the water. We do have an alibi, remember? From what I know, I think we are clear to call it in."

I sighed and looked around at the faces of the other men on the boat. This trip has turned out to be one of the most bizarre things that I had experienced in my life up to date. I didn't want to be involved in this anymore than any of the other men on this boat. But, I pulled out my cell phone and dialed 911 and prayed for better days ahead.

CHAPTER 16: MAINE

That phone call was just the start of what turned the tides of my professional career as I'd dreamt it. I still had about an hour to go before the plane touched down and my head was still reeling from the last four days. I had ordered a shot of Remy Martin XO about 5 minutes ago from the stewardess. I figured it would be the closest that I would come to feeling a release of all the tension I felt as a result of this last trip.

As I sat there rubbing my eyes and waiting on my liquid salve, I could have sworn that I felt somebody staring at me. I looked around and it appeared that everybody was minding their own business. I'm just paranoid, I thought. Sin has a way of making you feel that way. Even worse. I killed someone and that was not part of the plan. It was self-defense; right? Or, was it? I know that Rolando McLemore was onto the whole operation and it was going to be just a matter of time before the walls of the empire I'd help to build would come tumbling down on top of me. But, it all happened so fast! I don't even have all of the pieces to this puzzle that I find myself a part of.

It all started after my fourth visit to the Monterey plant. I had developed a slight rapport with Rosito; and, he was even beginning to crack a few jokes whenever I came through for my site inspections. However, I saw very little of Cyril, since he was overseeing the construction operations onsite; and that was still considered a restricted access zone. I figured that most of the people had been briefed on who I was and the reason for my visits. But, for the most part, I checked the books to make sure everything was on the up and up for the audit; which is conducted on a bi-annual basis.

Usually, I would spend an average of three to four days in Monterey in order to go over all of the processes that I am required to report on. Well, the other day, I had spent the early part of the morning going over all of the bookkeeping and trying to come up with ways to streamline some of our processes for cost-cutting purposes. I was getting a little tired of just going through numbers and figures; so, I decided to venture through the plant and inject a little field trip into my day.

I walked across the courtyard area and into another section of the plant that I never really noticed before. *What is this building for?* I wondered aloud as I strode towards it. It appeared not to have an entrance; upon the first glance. So, I came around to the side and noticed that there was a latch leading to the ground floor. I flipped the lock and noticed that it was already open. So, I pulled it up and stepped down into the dimly lit area. This area led down a corridor that seemed to be the second floor of what originally appeared to be a one story building. I kept walking and saw a bluish light emitting from a double door panel further down the hall. As I approached the blue light, I noticed that there were two small viewing panels along the top of the doorway. I stood on my toes and peered inside the room; intrigued by what I might find on the other side. As I looked through the panel, I saw several rows of people; an assembly line of workers in hard hats and goggles. As I looked more closely, I noticed that the workers were assembling phones and completing the packing process. *How odd!* I thought to myself. I know that we handle all of those processes out of the distribution center. *I wonder what is going on.*

At that moment, I saw a forklift in the distance approaching one of the tables towards the middle of the room. A couple of people helped take the inventory off the lift and began to unload a few boxes at each station. One of the team leads, as it appeared, cut open one of the boxes and took out several packets of a white powdery substance. Then, he took one of the P-10 model cellular casings and separated it; adding a foam interior, and then, placing one of the packets of the white powder on top of it. Then, he began packaging it by placing it in a lined box for shipping.

I couldn't believe what I was seeing! Just as I was about to turn away from the door, my pager went off! *OH SHIT!!* One of the Team Leads looked up when he heard the noise and started towards the door. I ran down the hallway as fast as I could. I could hardly see in front of me; which turned out to be to my detriment. I didn't see the small doorway on the side just before my exit panel. Before I knew it, I took a fist to the dome and I fell backwards and hit the floor. The next thing that I knew, I was being lifted from the floor and restrained. I must've blacked out some time after that because the next memory that I had was of me sitting in complete darkness in a locked room. I felt around for the light switch; which I never found, and waited in utter silence for someone to either rescue or kill me. I had no idea what time it was or how long I had been there. After what seemed like forever, Rosito came into the room accompanied by the burly man that had knocked me out on my ass.

"What the hell is going on?" I asked Rosito; shielding my eyes from the flare of the light that had entered the room.

"See, college boy, I told you that you were in over your head! I'm here to make sure that we can work this all out real peaceful-like. You had no business down here," Rosito sneered.

"Whatever man. Look. All I want to do is get out of here. I really don't care about whatever else you got going on up in here as long as you leave me out of it," I said half-heartedly.

"Well, son, that's part of the problem. I just can't let you walk out of here like ain't nothing happened. As far as I'm concerned, we've got us a little situation on our hands. You can't leave here until we get it fixed. Manuel? Take our friend here down to the cellar to see Cyril. I think he may have a way of helping us out with this mess," said Rosito to the burly dude.

With that, Manuel took hold of my arm and jerked me into a standing position.

"Now, walk!" Manuel barked as he shoved me from behind into the darkness.

I guess Manuel started to get impatient with me because he grabbed me by the arm, again, and started dragging me down the corridor. I thought about trying some break away moves that I had seen Marshall Faulk do during one of his stellar game performances; but, I thought better of it. What am I going to do? I figured it was best to just play it cool for now; especially if I wanted to get out of here alive...

Manuel opened a huge steel door and shoved me inside. Slightly off balance and unable to see in the dim lighting, I stumbled forward, fell over something lying in the floor and landed on my ass is front of Cyril.

"I see that you are not content enough to just mind your own business and do what your told," Cyril spat at me.

"Look, just like I told them, you can let me go and we can all walk away from this like nothing ever happened," I said to Cyril and his goons.

Cyril smiled and pulled out a cigar from his pouch. "I guess you realize that we can't do that; now, don't you? You know too much and knowledge is power in this business. That's a combination that we can't afford to have you wield over us. As far as I'm concerned, we need something that is going to level the playing field. Wouldn't you agree, Maine?"

I thought for a second; wanting desperately to craft a good, solid answer.

"I don't agree. But, I know that it makes no difference at this point."

"Well, thank you for your honesty, my friend. I want to introduce you to your fate. Manuel get Rolando," Cyril commanded.

Manuel walked over to a trap door in the floor and pulled someone out of it. I recognized him to be Rolando McLemore; one of the FBI Inspectors that had been conducting investigations at the site.

"Oh my God!" I heard myself scream. It was clear that Rolando had been smacked around quite a bit.

Cyril started, "See my man Rolando here? I tried to negotiate with him and all he kept giving me in return were threats; which I don't appreciate. Rolando interfered with one of my major shipments to Costa Rica; which cut into my budget for about 1.5 million. But, he made the mistake of trying to confront me about it before he went to his superiors with his information. I am NOT a man that favors confrontation."

"What does all this have to do with me?" I interrupted.

Rosito lunged forward and punched me in the stomach. "You sure don't have any manners for a college boy! Don't interrupt the man while he's talking!"

Cyril laughed, "That's okay, Rosito. The young man is eager for his assignment. I like to see that in our young executives. It shows heart. I'm going to give you all the tools you need to complete your assignment."

Then, Cyril tossed a sawed off shotgun at me. At that moment, I felt my knees buckle. *This is it,* I thought silently. *They want me to kill myself!* I continued to stand there and grip my fate. I wanted to cry; but I couldn't bitch up at a moment like this. So, I just stood there shaking.

"As you've already heard, we can't afford to have any dissension in our export operations. Frankly, that's too much money to have to part with without there being some serious circumstances. So, we are going to need your help in making this thing right," Cyril further explained. "So, I would like for you to take care of Rolando for us."

At that statement, I swallowed really hard. Finally, I said, "I can't do that Cyril..."

Manuel pulled out an assault rifle and aimed it right at my pelvic region.

"Then, we will kill you...slowly."

Now, as I saw my career and all of the things that I worked so hard to accomplish flash before my eyes, I began to have an epiphany. I am not a killer; but, there is no way I'm about to lose my nuts over this! As I contemplated my next move, I surveyed the room. All eyes were on me. I could see Rolando begging me through tear-stained eyes to think of something quickly. My head started spinning as I was running out of options. The next thing I know, I heard a gunshot, the sound of a body falling and my own lights went out! The last thing that I remembered was being dropped off at the airport with my return ticket home in my right hand; and, the reality that I am a wanted man as my most vivid mental picture.

CHAPTER 17: PHYLLIS

Feeling scared makes me want to have sex; and sex is what got me into this predicament in the first place. I can't believe that I have hurt Donna like this! But, in the back of my mind, I'm kind of mad at her for holding out on me with the fact that Jarrod is packing! *See what I mean?* I really need help. I'm so twisted up inside that I can't do nothing but cry. I think about all of the shit that I have been mixed up in and I cry even harder.

Every decision that I have ever made has had to do with sex in some way. I can hardly sit in my chair at work because it puts that "feel good" pressure on my clit. If I go grocery shopping, I spend an awfully long time in the vegetable section; near the cucumbers. If I go to the car wash to vacuum out my ride, I take the hose and put it between my legs before my last quarter runs out so that I can feel what super suction power is like. I am out of control and I have no idea how to stop it. The bad part about it all is that I can't even turn to my girls on this one.

If I tell Kia, she will shake her head, call me a hoe and forbid me to ever come by her house; whether she is there with Simeon or not. She will not want to take the risk. Ari will probably flip into counseling mode and analyze me well back into infancy. I don't want to deal with the criticism. What am I going to do? *I could kill myself! Yeah! That's it!* I can end all of my misery and never have to bask in the face of sexual ruin again! *How can I do it, though?* I could smother myself! I'll grab my Tempur-Pedic pillow and secure it over my head with some duct tape. This will be fool-proof! That way, the pillow won't move when I thrash around for air.

So, I went downstairs, got the tape and went to my bed to get the pillow. But wait! *Should I leave a letter to let everyone know that I am sorry for everything? That I have lost my will to live?* Naw. That would probably look too pathetic. *But what do I care about appearances?* I have already ruined any chances of having a decent reputation. Everyone that I meet is either someone I've slept with; or the friend or relative of somebody I've hit! I need to just get this over with right now. I'll cut the T.V. on so that I can distract my mind from focusing on my actions. I let the T.V. rest on some infomercial channel. I walked over to my computer desk, clicked it on and opened up a blank Word document. There was no need for proper alignment or the perfect font. One simple sentence would be sufficient:

My body, mind, soul and my actions were consumed by the freak within me…

Phyllis

So, I pushed print, tucked the note inside my shirt pocket (so it would be easy to find) and sat in the middle of the bed. I grabbed the pillow and the duct tape. I put the pillow to my face and unraveled the duct tape around my head with my free hand. I kept wrapping the tape tighter and tighter. I saw less and less rays of light. I began to feel a sense of peace as I let my mind wander. *What was waiting for me on the other side?* I can't wait to get there! I could feel my body tensing from the lessened oxygen flow to my brain. All of a sudden the television station changed abruptly.

OH Shit! I forgot that I set the timer to BET earlier in the day. The next thing I know, I hear Little Jon screaming, "WHAT! WHAT! OKAY!" What the hell? I can't leave this world with the King of Crunk as my theme music! So, I jumped up and tried to snatch the pillow/duct tape concoction from my head. But, there was a slight oversight on my part. Some of the duct tape had become secured in my hair. So, when I ripped off my death mask, I also ripped out a patch of hair from my roots! I screamed as my comforter became spotted with the blood from my scalp.

"I can't do anything right!" I screamed aloud to no one but myself; as I began to cry all over again. I was so mentally exhausted that I continued to cry until I finally cried myself to sleep.

I woke up and looked at the clock on the dresser. It was 3:42am. I rubbed my eyes; which hurt from all the crying I had done. I looked over at the T.V.; which was still playing. It was back to playing infomercials because it was so late. I just stared at the screen, aimlessly, for what seemed like an eternity. Then, a medical doctor came on the screen talking about various addictions and the work that her clinic had done on their behalf.

"Call the clinic, day or night. We will assist you in getting the help you need," the doctor was saying.

She had a kind face. It was the face of a nurturer; someone who actually cared about the welfare of those that she came into contact with. The number kept flashing at the bottom of the screen: 1-888-766-2105.

I felt like I had been thrown a life preserver as I picked up the receiver and reached out for the help that I so desperately needed.

CHAPTER 18: KIA

Everything is all set for tonight. I called Don Pablo's to have them bring the food over for the party that I'm throwing later. I really didn't feel like I should host an event after I spent time slaving over a stove.

I must say that I will be looking pretty, hot and tempting this evening! I permed my hair and sharpened my cut earlier this morning so that I wouldn't have any worries in the hair style department. I also made the run to the nail shop to make sure that I got my manicure and pedicure. I plan to wear a killah pair of open-toe stiletto heels and I don't want to take anything away from my look.

I ran down my list in my little pink book and invited everyone I knew. I'm glad that I nagged Simeon into cleaning the pool out before he left for his trip. The weather is going to be perfect all weekend and I plan on extending the party onto the pool area so that everyone can find something to do that they will enjoy. I even snuck a little money out of Simeon's account and bought extra swimsuits and trunks for those who didn't bring their own. I figured I would just take that extra step in being the best hostess possible. Thanks, baby!

Anyway, I have even come up with another way to take the party to further heights. I did a little research and found a massage parlor over in the business district that let me use 2 male and 2 female masseurs to work the party, as well. I had to pay a base fee (which I took from our joint account) and the clients will pay the rest for the services that they receive. So, they are going to set up four massage tables and 2 chairs, pool side, so that they can off whatever type of massage the party-goers might like. Isn't that a great idea? This is definitely going to be the best house party that anyone has been to in a long time; and I am so excited that I am the one throwing it!

I even had my bootleg CD hookup from the shop make me a few mixed CD sets. He guaranteed me that I had at least 9 hours of continuous jams before I would even have to think of repeating any. He burns the CD's himself; so, if I have the slightest problem tonight, that's his ass! I even worked the magic on my liquor hook up. I pulled our giant cooler out of storage and filled it with beer, wine coolers, soda, spritzers and any other beverages that could fit into it. I set it up alongside the pool for easier access. Plus, I figure with the weather being so great; everyone would eventually migrate outside before too long. I checked my watch and I had about twenty minutes to go before I would start to see my first guests arriving.

I went into the front room and started the music and the food had been set up about 10 minutes ago. I heard the doorbell; I guess that I have less time than I thought. I checked myself in the mirror one last time and then went and answered the door.

"Hey girl, I figured I would come and help you get everything together. This is my cousin, Rita," my friend Sherelle said as she gestured to the robust lady behind her.

Sherelle is usually the first one to show up at any of the events because she likes to check out the food spread. Now don't get me wrong, she's cool and all; but, she loves to get her eat on for free! From the looks of Rita, she hasn't pushed a plate back ever! But, fortunately, I have enough food to go around.

"Hello, Sherelle and Rita. Come on in. Everything is already set up in the kitchen and pool side. Help yourself," I said.

"Girl, thank you! I was hoping you would say that. I told Sherelle that I was running low on fuel and I was about to go into my reserve!" Rita laughed as she pushed her way past me to make her way towards the kitchen.

"Anyone made it here yet?" Sherelle asked as she surveyed the room.

"No; not yet. But, I am expecting everyone to start getting here any minute now."

It wasn't long before my prediction rang true. I spent the next twenty minutes going back and forth to the door greeting my guests. I had actually rounded up a pretty nice crowd; if I must say so myself! The music was flowing smoothly. I am so glad that I had Simeon wire those speakers from the house into the pool area. That way, the party keeps on going no matter where you are! Since it seemed like the flow of incoming guests had slowed, I figured it would be a good time to mingle.

"Kenny used to try to pull that shit on me, too. Every time he would go out with the fellas, he would call me around 3am and say that he was just too drunk to come home," my client Patrice was telling the group in the dining area. "The last time he did it, I was more than ready for his ass! When he pulled that shit 3 weeks ago, I told him to stay where he was because I was sleepy anyway from getting it on with his replacement!"

Katrelle piped up, "I hope you put him out after that."

"Naw, she couldn't have put him out after that because I saw them a week ago at the swap meet

149

holding hands and looking all family-oriented," Neesy commented snidely.

"First of all, I don't know what you think you saw; but, you didn't see that!" Patrice retorted.

I stepped in to diffuse the situation. I didn't need any broken furniture or hair pulling going on up in here.

"Ladies, how is it going in here? Sounds like a really good conversation," I said to try and divert their attention to me. "Neesy, could you come out to the pool and help me serve the drinks? I think we may need to add some more ice to the margarita machine."

Neesy said, "Whatever," as she got up and followed me out of the dining area.

As we passed the kitchen, I noticed that Sherelle and Rita were still in the kitchen holding it down. In fact, Rita must've felt downright at home because I saw her leafing through the refrigerator; pick up a bottle of spray cheddar cheese, lift it up to her mouth and pull the trigger! *Mental note to self: Throw out all spray cheese containers after the party is over.*

Neesy and I continued outside so that I could get her started making drinks. I mingled a little bit more and decided that it was time for me to relax a little and enjoy my own party. Not that I haven't been doing that all along; but, I was ready to try on one of those new swimsuits that I had purchased. I also picked out a really cute sarong and matching sandals with a 3 inch heel. I was dying to show up all the wanna-be divas in training when I suited up.

So, I scurried into the pool house to put on my ensemble. It was a beautiful red and orange one piece; with an extremely low cut back and a vamping' neckline to show off my twins. I look so amazing in it, too! I bought the matching sarong because I wanted to shield all of the men from my ass-ets.

I pulled the suit off the hanger and wiggled out of my top. I pulled out some baby oil and began to saturate my skin. I wanted to have that "wet look" before I even hit the water. So, I poured a generous amount into the palms of my hands and began to rub my legs. I began at my ankles; avoiding my feet because I didn't want my feet to be too slippery in my heels. I poured some more oil into my hands and began to work my mid-section; adding a little extra to cover my backside. That's all I need is to have an ashy ass! I grabbed the bottle one last time and began to saturate my arms and breasts. The oil felt so good! I went over my breast area a 3rd time when I heard someone speak from behind.

"I always used to love the way you did that."

My body froze in recognition. It had been at least six or seven years since I had heard his voice. I reached for the body towel hanging on the hook nearby to cover up my nakedness. I didn't move too swiftly because I wanted him to see all that he had missed out on over the years. I wrapped the towel around me as I turned around and stared at "him".

"Kia, baby, you are looking better than ever! I've really missed you," Maurice whispered to me.

Try as I might, I had to smile at that one. I knew that I was just as tight as ever; even better! It's just something about a man who has walked out on you giving you your props! Maurice and I used to date; heavily, before Simeon and I got together. I really loved Maurice's dirty draws! Seeing him again like this is both pain and pleasure.

"How did you get in? Who told you where I lived?" The questions rushed out of me.

"Actually, I've known how to find you for quite some time now. I just couldn't think of a way to face you before now. A friend of a friend received an invite and invited me to come along. So, I figured this was my chance."

"Well, I'm married now and you shouldn't be here," I said with conviction.

"I'm here. Your husband isn't...and, I know that you still think about me," Maurice smiled with his eyes.

I shot him the iciest look that I could muster. "That's where you're wrong! You need to leave now! We are way past the point of discussion."

With that, I put my hand to his chest to push him out of the pool house. But, Maurice had other plans for me as he grabbed my wrist and spun me around with my back to him. I could feel the pressure that was mounting in his sculpted jeans against my hip region.

"You know that it always turned me on when you fought! Now; be a good girl and let me see if you've kept it hot for me!"

Maurice held me in place with his left forearm as he foraged under my towel with his right hand. Since Maurice had my arms pinned, I twisted my body to get some leverage and bowed him in his abdomen.

"Damn, girl! I'm just kidding with you," he whined as he let me go. "I see that you're not up to a reunion right now; so, I'll check you later," he said as he darted out of the pool house and into the mixed company outside.

I finished putting my suit on and I looked at myself in the mirror. I wanted to make sure that my face wasn't giving way to the fear that I felt in my heart after seeing Maurice.

See, Maurice is one of those pieces of my past that has never been spoken of. Like I said before, we dated heavily before I met Simeon. Maurice was perfect; except for two things. The first would be the forced abortion of our child. Secondly, would be the repeated rapes that led to the conception. I was young and wanted to do what it took to keep such a good catch as Maurice on my arm. Not only was and is he fine; but, he was the son of a Senator; which meant he was more than financially stable.

All was good until he started forcing me to have sex with him. Believe me; it wasn't that I wouldn't have volunteered for the job because I did. But, Maurice only seemed to be interested in it when I wasn't in the mood to give it. This started happening more frequently in the last year of our relationship; just before I completed beauty school. He started to get physical with me whenever I looked like I wanted to turn him down sexually. He would slap me, punch me (not in the face), pin me down and force himself inside of me. Each time he did this, I felt like I had internal bruises for days; which made me even more reluctant to sleep with him the next time around. Well, this kept up...until one day my period was 2 ½ months late; and, I found out that we were having a baby. I remember that day like it was yesterday...

"Maurice, I really need for you to come over. Do you have some time? We really need to talk," I said into the receiver.

"Babe, what's up? I'm really busy right now. Can't you just tell me over the phone? It'll be much quicker that way."

Not wanting to do it like that, but out of other options, I proceeded. "I took a test and I'm pregnant with our baby."

Maurice quickly responded, "Okay, can you meet me at that office building on the corner of 10th and Caprice? Be there this afternoon around 4:30pm," and with that, Maurice disconnected the phone; leaving me perplexed.

So, I clock-watched until about 4:10pm and made the 20 minute drive over to the building. I parked behind Maurice's Acura TL and went up to the door of the building. *What is this place?* I thought as I searched for a sign or some indication of what type of place it was and why we had to meet here. As soon as I put my hand on the door handle, Maurice pushed the door open.

"Hey Babe, come on in."

I looked at him with a puzzled expression, "Why are we meeting here?"

"I got somebody that I want to introduce you to," Maurice said as he pulled me down the hall to a room in the far back.

When we walked inside, Maurice closed the door behind us and I swore I heard the lock click.

"Nice to meet you Kia. I'm Yairobi," the strange man said.

"Good to meet you also. What's going on?" I asked them both.

"Yairobi is my homeboy from medical school. He's going to take care of you," Maurice said calmly.

"Take care of me? I don't understand," I pleaded with Maurice.

Maurice was growing more agitated by the minute. "Look Babe, just take off your pants and put on this gown. Yairobi is going to fix our little situation. He's doing me a favor; now, just relax and he will be done soon."

My heart fell to the bottom of my feet. "But Maurice, we haven't even talked about any of this! What if I want to keep the baby?" I cried out.

"Well, that's not a choice that you will be making! I have moves that need to be made; and this is not a part of the plan! Now just get on the table so that we can get this over with."

I had to resort to begging because he had to be stressed and not realizing what he was about to do to us.

"Maurice, please. Let's just go sit down somewhere and talk…"

Maurice interrupted, "BITCH, GIT YO ASS ON THE TABLE! I'M TIRED OF PLAYING WITH YOU!

Then, he pulled out a 9 millimeter and smacked me on the back of my head! My heart broke into a thousand pieces at that very instant. *How could he do this to me? To us?* At that point, I got undressed, climbed on the table and let Yairobi do what he came to do. After it was all over, I was too weak to drive. So, Maurice drove me home, carried me inside and laid me in my bed. He must've come back later and dropped my car off because when I looked outside the next morning, it was there. I stayed home an entire week after that incident. I made up an excuse for missing my classes at the beauty school so that they would let me make up what I missed while I was out. I never heard from Maurice after that, and that hurt me even more. I vowed to bury that memory deep inside the recesses of my mind; as though it were all a dream. I never even told Simeon about Maurice or the baby that I lost because it never quite came up. Plus, I didn't see the point in making him look at me differently because of it. So, after all these years, I have kept this secret.

Well; one last look in the mirror before I get back to my guests. I do have a party to attend to...

CHAPTER 19: ARI

Hunter and I climbed into his Volvo S60 and headed into the entertainment district on the other side of town. Along the way, we spent time catching up on what's been going on in each other's lives over the last 6 months; since the hiatus began. It feels good to be with him right now; talking and sharing. Hunter has always been a good listener and genuinely a good person, overall. I really have missed him. However, I cannot let on to him just how much.

We pulled into the Le Blanc Hotel valet station to have the car parked. Hunter jumped out and pulled what looked like an overnight bag from the trunk. How presumptuous of him! I hope he doesn't think that just because I agreed to come over here with him that I have reneged on my earlier statement! I got out of the car with an attitude and stood just inside the door of the lobby with my arms folded while he finished his business with the valet. Then, he came inside the lobby to join me.

"Do you mind waiting right here while I go up and check on things?" Hunter asked.

I responded tightly, "Hunter, you better not be playing any games with me. I told you that I didn't come up here for that type of visit."

Hunter continued to smile as he stroked my inner arm. "Ari, you know that I know better than that. I just want to check on a little something and I will be right back."

And with that, he hit the elevator up button and was gone. I took this opportunity to people watch and pray that it wasn't going to take him long to finish checking on whatever it is. I sat down on the bench off to the right of the main lobby; but, in plain view of the elevators. I didn't want to take the risk of being seen by anyone who might question why I was in the hotel during work hours on a work day. I should have dressed more conservatively so that I could at least feign a business meeting. Oh well! A couple of people scurried in and out of the lobby before Hunter finally returned to my side.

"You ready?" He grinned expectantly.

I said nothing as I stood and walked over to the elevator corridor. We stepped inside and he pushed the stop button.

"Just before we go any further, I would like for you to wear this," he said as he reached into his duffle bag and pulled out a black silk eye mask.

I regarded it with skepticism before reaching for it.

"No, let me do that for you," Hunter said as he stood behind me to secure the mask over my face. "I always remember how much you love surprises."

I couldn't deny that. I do love a good surprise! I had to admit that I was more than mildly curious about what was happening on the floors above. I felt the elevator start again and we rose for what seemed like a small eternity. Then, I heard it chime and felt the wind rush in as the doors opened. I was greeted by the faint scent of mangoes and jasmine. Hunter grabbed me by the hands and led me out of the elevators into the area of surprise. When he removed the eye mask, I audibly gasped. The setting was so beautiful! We were on the roof of the hotel; which had to be at least 40 stories high. There was greenery everywhere and the most exotic flower arrangements that I had ever seen lining the edges of the rooftop. In the center of it all, there was a marble dining table set for two. I couldn't believe that this was all done just for me!

"OH Hunter! Why did you do this? It's all...just so...wonderful!"

Hunter replied, "Ari, I would do this and much more for you if you give me the chance. I want you to know how much I really value what it is that we have together."

With that statement, Hunter took my face in the palm of his hands and looked deeply into my eyes.

"Just for this night, I have composed an original poem to let you know what is in my heart. I call it 'The Past 6 Months'.

These past six months you have weighed heavily on my soul.
I sit in a daze; keeping me in constant thought.
In constant thought of what we have shared and what we could share in.

I've grieved for your touch.
Your smile.
Your scent.
You are my drug; and I your fiend
I ache for your grasp of my manhood
I hunger for your taste
I crave you.

These past six months have been unbearable.
Ari, I want to close the gap
I want you and only you.
I need you
I have to have you
Ari, you are my high; and, I can't live without you.

I began to cry. I didn't know what other emotion to feel at that time except a mixture of both joy and regret. I have always wanted a man to profess his undying love and devotion to me. I just never imagined that it would be someone else's man. But, as if he were reading my thoughts, Hunter began to speak as he wiped away my river of tears.

"I'm leaving her, Ari. I can't stand to go on, like this, another minute. When you called and wanted to meet with me earlier today; it was like destiny. Our second chance. I have something to prove to you how serious I am about us."

Hunter beckoned for a waiter that I hadn't realized had been standing over in the corner. He brought a silver platter, with a lid, up to Hunter and lifted it for him to remove the contents. Hunter pulled out an envelope and handed it to me.

"Open it," he said.

I did. There was a one-way ticket with my name on it bound for Tahiti. I was confused and elated, simultaneously.

"What am I supposed to do with this?" I asked.

Hunter answered solemnly, "If you feel only half of what I do for you; you are supposed to accept it and board the plane tonight. I will finish tying up the remaining loose ends with the lease on my office space, get some of my things and meet you there. I'm asking you to run away with me."

I couldn't believe what I was hearing. Of all the fairy-taleish things in the world! I hope he is not serious.

"How can you expect me to just pack up and run off with you on a moment's notice? I do have a life here, Hunter. A full life at that," I reminded him. "I really hate to end the dream for you; but, what about your wife? I know you don't think that she is going to just let you ride off into the sunset and leave her with your kids. You're not being very realistic."

Hunter showed no signs of faltering. "I have already taken care of everything. I will miss my children; but, I am going to take better care of them this way. I don't expect for you to understand all of the details; but, I can assure you that I have covered all of my bases. You don't have to worry about your job; since you work remotely, anyway. You can still do your graphic designing from there. Just pack a few things and board the plane. That's all I'm asking. For me. For us."

Moments later, we were back in Hunter's Volvo headed back to the café so that I could retrieve my car. My head was still reeling from all of the excitement of the evening. I still couldn't believe that the fat lady hadn't sung on this one yet. It was all a dream; yet, I was wide awake... Tahiti, here I come?

CHAPTER 20: SIMEON

Why is it no matter where you are in the world, there is always a card-carrying member of the good old boy network associated with police work?

"Now, which one of you boys allegedly found the body?" Officer Thims asked us after having arrived on scene and waiting on the coast guard to help him drag in the body.

David spoke first, "I did. I was in the water and I saw the bag with the hand sticking out of it."

Officer Thims looked us all over and his eyes landed on Moteif.

"What about you, Rasta man? What part did you play in all this? Or, were you to busy smoking reefer?"

Moteif's eyes burned with hatred. "Who the fuck you talking to?"

Officer Thims jumped at the sound of his voice. "Boy, you better watch yourself. I just asked you a simple question. Now, answer it!"

"I'm not your boy," Moteif said in a challenging tone. "I suggest that you call for some more back up. You're gonna need it to pull me off of your ass!"

"Officer, we are all upset because this is not the way that we were expecting our fishing trip to turn out. I hope you understand that. If you will just give us a minute to talk with our friend," I said in hopes of quelling the brewing riot.

"I'm not letting you all talk where I can't hear it. What do you think I am, stupid? So, you just gone have to rely on the account that you all have probably made up before I got here!" Officer Thims spat at us.

I truly must say this situation was escalating quickly. I was starting to see that we would not be getting out of this thing with our pride in tact. I felt like the officer was just trying to antagonize us so that he could have an official reason to haul us in on charges. After all, it was his account against ours and we were the strangers in town.

"Just chill, Moteif," Cashon pleaded with him on the entire group's behalf.

"No more talking! What the hell type of gang message you passing, boy?" Officer Thims shot in Cashon's direction.

"Nothing sir. I was just asking him to relax," Cashon responded.

"Well speak English, nigga! Ain't that another one of your terms of endearment?" Officer Thims remarked snidely.

"You cracker mothafucka!" Moteif shouted as he charged full speed at the officer.

The next thing I know, Moteif is on top of Officer Thims, beating the hell out of him! Thims was trying to scrap back; but not so successfully. Then, as if in slow motion, I saw the gun slide from the holster.

"BANG! BANG!"

Moteif fell away from Officer Thims with a look of surprise on his face. But, Officer Thims was lying there, still, with two shots oozing from his chest cavity.

"Oh My God! Moteif, what have you done man?" David hollered at Moteif.

"It was an accident, man! Ya'll all saw it, right? He tried to shoot me for nothing!" Moteif clamored.

"How are we gonna explain this to the Port Authorities?" Cashon asked everyone. "Remember, they are on their way and we now have one extra dead body!"

"I can't believe this shit, Moteif. All you had to do was calm the fuck down and you couldn't even do that! Now we all going to jail!" I said.

I just couldn't believe how fast everything spiraled from bad to worse in just a matter of minutes. All I could see now was me sharing a cell with my new boyfriend Nate. How the hell was I going to explain this in my one phone call to Kia? Fuck it, I can't risk this thing getting any worse on my behalf. So, I whipped out my cell phone and dialed 911.

"911 Emergency Response. How may I assist you?" the operator replied.

"I'd like to report an accident. We already called in once to report finding a dead body during a boating expedition in Baja, California. I would now like to report that the responding officer has been shot, also." I told her.

Before I could hear the beginning of her response to me, Moteif jumped up in my face and knocked my cell phone out of my hand and into the water below.

"Are you crazy? What the fuck is your problem, Simeon? You trying to get me sent up or something? We haven't discussed our game plan yet and you all up on the phone trying to absolve yourself from this shit!" Moteif squared off with me.

"Look man. You created this mess. I am just trying to make sure that the facts stay straight," I said; wondering what the hell had gotten into Moteif. Sure, he was always different from the rest of us; but, I was suddenly not feeling this thug bravado that he was putting forth at such a critical time.

Moteif grabbed the gun, aimed it at my head and cocked it. "The only thing straight around here is going to be your outline on the floor of this boat if you don't shut the fuck up!"

Now, I am nobody's punk. I know that Moteif and I go way back. But, I'll be damned if he is going to pull a gun on me; and, especially not in front of David, Cashon and Carl; who have all been exceptionally silent throughout most of this exchange. Not only had he shown that he had lost his mind by talking crazy to me and putting a gun to my head; but, he started taunting the other guys, too.

"What the fuck ya'll looking at? Everybody has lost their nuts now, huh? I feel like it's 'Dre Day' up on this boat! Who's the man with the master plan? Come on, don't act like ya'll don't know the rest!" Moteif continued to heckle the group.

Clearly, someone had to make a move to slow this clown's role. He was definitely certifiable now! I looked over at the rest of the guys to see what page they were on. David looked like he was holding a private prayer vigil. Cashon looked scared as hell. Carl was looking in the vicinity of a pole that was tucked in the inner frame of the boat off to his right. I gave him the unspoken go-ahead to get to it quickly. Carl took the go-ahead and ran with it! With lightening speed, he was on his feet (pole in hand) and swung in one swift motion; knocking Moteif off of his feet.

But, before Moteif went down, he must have glimpsed Carl coming for him. The gun went off and suddenly everyone was scrambling for cover as the Port Authorities siren blazed its nearness. This had to be the darkest moment of my life, yet.

CHAPTER 21: MAINE

A man on the lamb has to follow his routine and not appear out of the ordinary; which is why I had to get on the plane and head towards home, as scheduled. I have to get my affairs in order; and, I really don't know what my next move is going to be.

Hopefully, the one person in the world that I can trust will understand what I have to do now. Ari will know that I had no other choice. I was a man without options. I tried calling her when my plane landed; but, I got her messaging system on both her home and her cell phones. *Maybe she's still hard at work on the Henderson Project.* I know that we were supposed to meet up and go over the specifics for the meeting in the morning; but, needless to say, there has been a change in plans.

As cloudy as my mind is, I was doing a lot of thinking about my next move. I don't want to leave a lot of people in the lurch as far as my whereabouts are concerned. But, I can't see them just letting me go back to the way things were before this all happened. I already know that my job is obsolete at this point. They've probably done everything that they could to cover their asses and to leave mine out to dry.

Let's see? There's a dead man; and me at the other end of the trigger. It won't take a rocket scientist to figure this one out. Plus, I know I'll look equally as crazy trying to explain myself to the authorities. Sure, they will be understanding and sympathetic to my plight; just long enough to lure me into custody...And that ain't happening! I'm just going to have to fight this thing on the run.

I know when my parents find out it is going to kill them, literally. All of their energies invested-for this. All of my accomplishments pale in comparison to a murderous rap sheet. *How could this have all gone so wrong?* I began to cry as I drove along the streets; trying to figure out my next move. My head ached as I toiled, mentally, to figure a way out of this mess. My headache worsened each time I continued to come up empty.

I cried even harder at my own desolation. It seemed as though with each tear, my feet grew heavier and heavier on the accelerator. The increased speed served as my get away from the present. I shot past the residential areas just beyond the airport. I continued to drive, at an increased rate of speed, until I reached the rural outskirts of town. I had no idea where I was headed; but, I had a pretty good idea of the places that I wasn't about to visit.

It was pitch black outside; as this side of town had very little street lighting. I didn't care. I continued to drive at break-neck speed. I didn't even chance looking in my rear view mirror for fear that the recent past was in hot pursuit of my present. I continued to think about the current state of my affairs. I guess I was so absorbed in my own problems that I didn't have enough time to react to whatever it was that ran across my path in the road. I swerved at the last minute to miss it; but I lost control of the car! I was on a two lane stretch of highway ascending into the hills; a part of town that is referred to as The Peak.

As I struggled to regain control of the car, I realized two things. First of all, I was going way too fast to come to a safe halt. Secondly, I heard the sound of metal tearing as I hit the external median and went over the edge of the cliff!

All at once, I was gripped by fear; followed by a startling calm. In that short span of time, I reflected on the things that mattered most to me. I fingered the letter addressed to Ari; which was located in the right breast pocket of my suit coat.

After that, my reality faded into non-existence.

CHAPTER 22: PHYLLIS

Today is the day. I am checking into the Pogner House to begin the second stage of my recovery. The first stage, as I was told over the phone, was recognizing the fact that I have a problem; and, that I need help in order to deal with it and move on with my life.

I couldn't sleep a wink last night as I thought back on my life and how much of a mess I've made of things. I just can't believe that it all boiled down to this. To finally put a name tag on this thing has made me feel a little better. Sexual addiction is one of those illnesses that most people don't even regard as something to be addressed; more like undressed. Society promotes promiscuity. The more things you get away with, the more depraved you become.

The other thing that I'm struggling with is the fact that I have hurt others while indulging in my own vaginal fantasies. The countless faces that I've bedded. Anybody's man, somebody's husband, relatives *(I've literally scaled family trees for God's sake!).* And, I'm banned from the church because everybody knows about what happened between Donna and me when I slept with her husband, accidentally. For everybody to be so Christ-like, they sure are a judgmental bunch!

Anyway, I won't worry about that now. I have to get my affairs in order before I leave. When I registered over the hotline, they had me to sign onto the computer and take an entrance exam. It consisted of a lot of questions about my background, my lifestyle and my professional ventures. Then, towards the end, it got more intrusive with specific questions about my sex life. How often? How many? What's the largest number of people that you've slept with in one day? *Geesh!* I wanted to lie on some of the questions. Kind of make myself look a little better on paper than what I actually am. But, I figured what's the point? They probably have sexual history cops that pounce on you publicly for doing stuff like that!

Once I finished the exam, it gave me a print out of my agenda in the program. I was actually surprised that it didn't give me a scoring range to compare myself to. You know,

50-65 You are President of Hoeville
49-30 You are a member of the Cabinet; a direct report to the President of Hoeville

Instead, it gave me an agenda for my "stages" over the next 10 weeks. My rating must really be high for them to want to keep me on lock down for 10 weeks in the drying unit!

I now have a whole different set of issues with which to confront. *First, what do you pack to wear on sexual lock-down?* Everything I own oozes my ultra-femininity! What *do I tell my boss?* I think I can stall him by using FMLA and feigning a "family" emergency. I don't want everybody at the job all up in my business. Plus, it would be too awkward for me when I returned to work. Everyone would start hawking me; waiting for me to relapse. It could be as simple as seeing someone eating a banana as a snack and off I go! One wrong move and its solitary confinement! But, that's the type of thought process that I'm working to change because I can and will beat this thing!

I finally got everything together and packed for my stay. I decided to go business casual for my days and dressy casual for my evenings/night time. I felt like I should keep my look together just in case we have mixers or socials to go to at night. What? It's not like I intended to go cold turkey! I just want to be able to tame it down a little bit. Let me make sure that I haven't forgotten anything:

1. Put all my bills on auto pay
2. Left message for my boss and talked to HR representative. Already signed my papers for my leave of absence.
3. Left messages for Kia and Ari telling them I was going out of town on an extended assignment.

I realized when I heard their voices on their machines that I wasn't going to be able to tell them. I don't want to further tarnish the image that they have of me; especially when I am so serious about turning this thing around. I plan on telling them one day. On a day that we will all be sitting at a bistro table at a café; chatting like Sex-In-The-City throwbacks. They will tell me how I got my stuff together and how proud they are to have me as their friend. Then, I will open up and share my struggle and how I got over! But, until that day comes, I am keeping my mouth shut because I know that they don't have the level of understanding that it takes to really know what I'm going through. I sigh at the magnitude of the steps that I have to go through just to put my life into perspective. But, it will all be over soon. I just have to keep the bigger picture in mind.

I went next door to see Serenda, my neighbor, who will be watching my house for me while I "visit family" for the next 10 weeks. I gave her the extra keys and other instructions and asked that she leave some lights on and make the place look lived in until I returned. After I left Serenda's, I finished loading the car with all of my luggage, pulled on my floppy hat and matching tan sunglasses and jumped in the car headed for the Pogner House. I had already pre-selected my choice for riding music: DJ Quik's Balance and Options album. I figured that this would keep my head bobbing and my mind focused on the task at hand. The ride took about an hour and 45 minutes; but, it seemed much shorter.

The Pogner House is located just off the main road and is flanked by rolling hills and thick forestry. If one didn't know better, they might mistake it for a 5-Star Resort with its 18 hole golf course, Olympic-sized outdoor pool and tennis courts visible beyond the foliage. I wasn't sure where to put my car; so, I pulled into a lot across the street; about a block down from the house. I stepped out of the car and suddenly was hit with the warm sun and a renewed feeling of rejuvenation in my bones! I popped open my trunk and began unloading my luggage. I am so glad that I had most recently invested in the stackable kind with the straps to hold everything down! I closed the trunk, extended my luggage wheels and set off toward my future. Just as I got halfway across the street, my cell phone vibrated in my purse. I reached down and whipped it open without looking at the caller ID; vowing silently that this would be the last call that I would take before entering the facility.

"Hello?" I said.

There was about 5 seconds of awkward silence; then, I heard a sound that I couldn't quite make out growing in the distance.

"Bbbb.......iiiiiiiiiiiiiiiiiiii....ITCH!" the caller screamed into the receiver.

At that moment, I heard the squealing of tires and looked up in time to see the truck that was headed right for me! I tried to haul ass; but, my legs wouldn't move. As the truck was only inches from my body, I saw Donna's snarling face grow even more contorted as she floored the pedal!

"BOOMP!" went my body and luggage as the truck collided into my frame.

My body was immediately racked with pain as I fought to remain conscious. I couldn't move my arms; as I was trying to will them to reach for my cell phone to call an ambulance. I laid there fighting back tears as I silently cursed the death angel for coming to visit all too soon.

"Please Lord, don't let it end this way!" I prayed silently as I lay on the asphalt.

This was my final conscious thought.

CHAPTER 23: KIA

The party is a complete success if I must say so myself; and, I do! It is always a challenge to pull a party together and make it look like it took little or no effort to pull it all off. I just finished ushering out my last guests, Rita and Sherelle. It was pure hell convincing them that I was all out of food to eat!

As I shut the door behind them, I slipped my hands under my top and slipped out of my bra. Whew! Now that's what being comfortable is all about! I strolled out into the backyard to the pool house to collect all the wet suits, cut off the lights and lock it down for the night. I decided to leave the stray glasses and plates till in the morning. I really am tired and I don't want to get caught up in cleaning mode and end up still on my feet, slaving, at 4am. I threw all of the suits in the washing machine and headed to the bathroom to jump in the shower. I undressed and showered for about 15 minutes; which is long enough for most of my hot water to run out on me.

So, I finished up, put a leave-in silkening conditioner in my hair and put an all-over body moisturizer on my skin. *I am now officially ready for bed,* I thought silently as I slipped into my favorite silk nightie. I turned the stereo on to listen to one of the jazz stations and hit the light as I climbed into bed. I know that I was already tired, so, I wouldn't have any trouble getting to sleep. But, I love to listen to music before bed; which usually disturbs Simeon.

So, I decided to take advantage of his absence and do something that I, alone, thoroughly enjoy. I slipped under the covers and quickly slid into dream mode. I immediately was transformed to a tropical island, complete with warm sun, sparkling black sand and a bevy of fine-ass men strolling leisurely along the shore. *Now, this is my kind of island!* I thought to myself as a couple of glances around told me that I was the only woman around; and, that all the men were casting flirtatious looks my way as I lay, exposed completely, seaside.

The realization hit me, at this point, that I really must be tired because I have not had anything remotely close to an erotic dream in quite some time. As the men passed, I made eye contact with each one. I, then, spread my legs open and began to perform a rhythmic two-finger massage of my labia.

Each man; each one finer than the one before him, would slow their pace and stare hungrily at my fountain of love. The attention made me spread my legs even wider, throw my head back and let the sun add to the growing heat emanating from my body.

As I continued to move my fingers in slow circles, I felt my nipples harden. *I don't want to do this by myself,* I thought. As if they read my mind, two of the men kneeled beside me and began sucking my nipples and stroking my exposed flesh. I heard myself moan as the intensity of all of our actions grew in unison. Each of the passersby stared more intently as they each whispered, "Come for me," as they stroked themselves gently. I couldn't take it anymore as I watched the endless parade of men begging me to take the next step for them. Suddenly, my two assistants flipped me over. Then a new man slid under me and entered me slowly as he sucked my nipples alternately and expertly. I released small gasps of pleasure as I relished how good this mystery man was putting it down! As if this wasn't working, I felt someone nuzzle me from behind, kneading my breasts as they were being suckled by the other man.

"I have wanted to do this for so long," the second man whispered as he tunneled his way in for back entry.

I shook visibly and cried out in ecstasy as I have never done before. I was the star of my own porn movie-minus the cameras-and I was being turned out! As these two dicks collided inside of me, I heard both men say, "There's a freak within all of us...set it free!

With that, I gave up the most intense orgasm I have ever had in my life; followed by two more just like it! My body convulsed so uncontrollably that it snatched me from my dream.

In one defining moment, my intense pleasure turned to pain as he stroked my hair, kissed my neck and said, "That's the way to welcome Maurice home, baby..."

CHAPTER 24: ARI

"Here is your pillow, Ms. Clayton," the stewardess said as she placed it behind my head.

The seven hour flight probably wasn't going to be long enough to clear my head from all of the activity that had surfaced from the previous evening. I still can't believe that I am sitting on a plane, bound for Tahiti, on a whim from a married man! But, I am more focused on the fact that it is more about me than it is about him. I have always been one who loves to take risks; but, I have a preference for calculated ones. In the scheme of things, this doesn't really make the most logical sense. I thought about calling Kia and Phyllis to run it by them to insure my own insanity; but, I thought better of it. The only judgment I am using at this point is my own. Sometimes, you just get tired of using sound reason as the basis of all of your decision-making. For once, I am following my heart and getting the hell on with my life! I have experienced numerous encounters waiting on at least one of those experiences to produce a relationship of substance.

Now, I am on a plane destined for an island that holds the key to my new existence! I packed relatively light; per Hunter's request. I figured that I could just send for the remainder of my things later. Just before take off, I tried calling Maine to let him know that I flaked on the Henderson Project; and, for him to try to stall on it for at least another week when I am settled and can devote all my energies towards it. But, I got his voicemail; so I opted for an extended message reiterating those points. I know he is going to cuss me out when he finds out what I have done. But, I plan to floss it over and my job; as opposed to the intense yearning of my heart. Before we parted, Hunter told me that he would join me in Tahiti by week's end. That will give me enough time to begin touring the island for sights, as well as looking for the area that we will make our home. I plan to check out all the night life, drink every kind of beverage that has an umbrella in it and relax for the next five days. As I closed my eyes and settled into my pillow, I envisioned palm trees, waterfalls and sunny days until I fell asleep.

I took a cab from the airport to the Chamblain Hotel. It's a 4-Star hotel set in the mountains; overlooking the heart of the island. I fell in love instantly with the scenery as we drove the winding path leading to my destination. I checked in and was informed that I had a message. The Concierge handed me the phone and I blushed as I heard Hunter's voice telling me how much he loved me and how much it killed him to wait those five days outside of our paradise. I tipped the worker for delivering the message that uplifted my day and was off to my room. It along with the rest of my property was gorgeous! I arrived just in time for dinner; so, I called downstairs to order room service.

"Ms. Clayton, your every meal has been pre-selected over the next five days compliments of your gracious sponsor," the gentleman informed me.

How presumptuous, yet playa of Hunter, I thought aloud. Then, the chef further informed me of the times each meal delivery; minus the contents.

"I am afraid that my staff and I are under direct orders not to divulge the contents of your meals; but to simply delight your palette with each offering," he continued.

I must admit that I was more than amused at this current display. Hunter had simply outdone himself

this time! It has covered every detail; which makes me long for his presence even more than I did originally. So, over the next five days, I received my breakfast in bed, my lunch at the Hotel Bistro and my dinners by candlelight out on the terrace. I grew increasingly fond of dinner because it was always accompanied by a handwritten declaration of love from Hunter. My days were filled with catching the sights and scenery; and my nights were filled with loneliness because I missed Hunter so much! I tried to go out and hit the town on a couple of occasions, but my heart nor my head, simply wasn't into it enough to make a good time of it.

On day number five, I received a telegram from Hunter stating that there had been a delay. *A delay?* What the hell kind of message is this? I was fuming as I raced back to the room to dial his cell phone number. I have been waiting on his ass for at least a week and all the information he can manage to provide is that there has been a delay? Oh, hell naw! So, I grabbed my phone, hit the speed dial and waited on an answer.

"Hello?" a female voice answered.

"Is this Cherise?" I asked to mask my surprise as his wife answered the phone.

"No, it isn't," she said.

"Sorry, must be the wrong number," I finished as I hung up even hotter than I was before.

What the hell is Hunter trying to pull? Even though I was so pissed off I couldn't see straight, I decided to try to clear my mind and take a jog along the island. About a mile into my jog it became a sprint; and beyond that, it was more like a full-fledged marathon. My body gave out somewhere in the beginning of the fourth mile and I collapsed into the sand along the shore. That's when my thoughts caught up to my mind. *Had Hunter made a fool of me? How could I have opened myself up like this again?* The only good part about it was that I didn't have to face anyone else looking like a fool. The agony lies in the fact that as soon as I looked in the mirror, I would greet the fool I had become; face-to-face. DAMN! I cried softly as I gathered enough strength to pull myself upright and walk back in the direction of the hotel.

About forty-five minutes later, I made it to the room; drained physically and emotionally. I jumped into the shower to freshen up, wrapped my hair and plugged in my laptop. Isn't it funny how you never know how much you'll miss something until you don't have it right at your fingertips? I had that exact feeling two nights ago when I suddenly wanted to see some U.S. news and find out what was going on in the world. My T.V. in the hotel wouldn't cooperate; however, because all of the

local news was in the local dialect. So, I plan to remedy that by checking out CNN and the California Sun Times via the World Wide Web. CNN held its usual commentary regarding killings, shootings and espionage. I quickly flipped through my local paper in hopes of something less tragic. My heart stopped as I read the caption under the following headline:

Man Arrested in Attempt to Stage Own Death: Police Arrest Hunter Morgan in Insurance-related Scam

CHAPTER 25: SIMEON

I never thought that I would see the inside of a jail cell. It is amazing how much life can change, so drastically, in just the blink of an eye. Even though the whole thing was clearly self-defense, I still have to await my bond hearing. I used my one call to phone my wife, Kia, and tell her the news. I dreaded making the necessary call and to my surprise, Kia did not answer the home phone or her cell. I left a message for her to contact our lawyer and have him come to the California State Municipal Court building to find out all of the particulars so that I can get the hell out of here. I also asked Kia not to tell Casey-Marie just yet. I wanted to wait until I was bonded so that I could explain everything to her myself. I feel like it will be better if the information comes from me directly; instead of trying to figure out the details from a third party.

I am still tripping on how everything went down. When Carl knocked Moteif off his feet, he knocked the gun out of his hands and I caught it and shot Moteif in the head! Carl, David and Cashon were initially detained by Port Authorities for questioning on all three dead bodies. Their stories must have been in sync because all three of them were released. Because I was the shooter of at least one of the victims, I was placed in a 6 x 9 to chill with my thoughts. *Man, this is fucked up!* I should have stayed my ass at home and avoided all of this shit! I feel like I'm in solitary confinement the way I'm isolated from everyone.

My mind is not my best companion right now. All I keep seeing are Moteif's dying eyes locked on mine as he took his last breath. I remember the Port Authorities coming in over the bullhorn telling me to drop my weapon. I recall them storming the boat, catching a couple of knees to my back and then, receiving my own pair of matching silver bracelets. I have never done time before and I'm starting to break out in a cold sweat from the mere thought, alone.

I've also received some real sub-par treatment from the staff since I got here. I think that some of the initial officers on the scene must have spread the word that I had possibly taken down one of their own. True enough, Officer Thims deserved a swift kick in the ass for his actions; but, he didn't deserve to die.

Now, I'm scared to eat because I swear the first meal that they brought me had shards of glass in it. There is nothing shiny about a meat patty and mashed potatoes! I'm scared to sleep because I have heard curdling screams coming from single-cell inhabitants like myself. That's the kind of thing that will keep a man awake forever; if need be...I have got to get the hell out of here.

Where the hell is my wife??

ACKNOWLEDGEMENTS

First and foremost, I would like to thank God for the creative energy and mental stability (or lack thereof) that enabled this project to be seen through to its completion. I would like to send a special "thanks" to my partner-in-literary-crime: Tracy J. Cass. Thank you for the reads, rereads, rewrites and constructive criticism that has led us to this; one of our finest moments. **Ivy Pyramid Forever!!**

Thank you to my husband, Jason, for making this book his only reading priority.
To my parents: LouCelia Courtney and Nuby G. Courtney (For this is the connection that made it all possible; and, they are the people that read to me before I could write). To my sister, Stephanie; who never judged me (out loud) and has always been one of my strongest supporters. Both of my nieces: Ceara Lynna and Saella; for the hours of

constant joy. To my stylist, Annette Bell (Hair-nette's Salon); for your years of dedication to my hair and for always being a true friend to me. My extended family: (Valla/Vernis/Matthew/Patrick), Oweida Carter, Jabbar Davis, Trina Williams (Holmes), Crystal Scott, Reginald Peel, Tangela Carter, Kevin Mondy, Dhara Tipler, Brian Cox, Uncle Sterling (one of my favorite uncles in the world), Larry Coleman Sr., Brett Taylor and The Cosmopolitan Bistro Family, The IBSH and the most understated musical phenom DJ Quik-You all fall into a special group! I would also like to extend a special thanks to my Illustrator, Pat Cass, for transforming my words into art. Thank you to Bryce Funderberg (Kaos Factor) for carrying the vision one step further.

There are a whole host of people/organizations that have shaped my overall development over the years; and I would like to extend my gratitude to you all from the bottom of my heart. I fear that in an attempt to list you all, I will leave someone/something out inadvertently-Please charge it to my head and not my heart! Just know that from Pine Bluff, Arkansas to the

DFW Metroplex, there is a trail of memories emblazoned upon my heart, eternally.

I appreciate each and every one of my supporters; as well as the naysayers-For w/o them there would be no fuel to the fire that propels me onward and upward.

In closing, I ask that you take the time to reflect on the foundation upon which Ivy Pyramid Publishing was founded:

Building literate minds...One book at a time...

SEE YA FOR BOOK #2: <u>Tales of a Good Girl</u>!

I

Printed in the United States
34114LVS00003B/76-102